CHOSEN LOVE

BLAZIN' LOVE BOOK FOUR

JA'NESE DIXON

PUBLISHING

Blazin' Love (Contemporary Romance)

Platinum Love (Book 1)

Privileged Love (Book 2)

Exclusive Love (Book 3)

Chosen Love (Book 4)

Special Love (Book 5) (Coming June 2019)

Steamy Sensations Holiday Love

ISBN-13: 978-1-950405-05-3 (paperback)

Printed in the United States of America.

One night...new heights...new lows...new love.

It's Memorial Day.

I had a simple plan. Find a decent guy, get married, have some babies. He didn't have to wow me, just a nice, normal, safe man. But my safe selection came with strings, and suddenly my simple plan isn't what I want at all.

I'm Taylor Wallace. I'm questioning life right now. Whether it's time to cut my losses and swap Plan A for Plan B. Thankfully, I have a great distraction. I joined my best friends in starting a new business, Platinum Prestige, an elite concierge service.

Then I meet Zach. His eyes see through my doubts, and his ironclad will steamrolls through my fears. He's everything I don't need, yet everything I want. But he's not part of my plan.

Our undeniable passion turns my simple life from black and white to vibrant color. It has me wondering why I ever settled for safe at all.

Then suddenly, my walk on the wild side lands me squarely in his trap...for life. And once again I'm torn between safe and reckless...settling and chosen.

What's a woman to do?

CHAPTER 1

*B*aby mama drama is the worst kind of drama.

"Fourteen years. Gone. Just like that." I nurse my weak drink checking my watch for the millionth time. I kicked Les' lying, cheating, trifling ass out of my house after his daughter's mother, Jovonta, came to *my house* dropping bombs bigger than Hiroshima.

I look up and find the waitress leaning into her hip with major attitude.

"Would you like anything?"

"I'm good." She wants this booth empty for the next customer, but I need to burn another hour because I don't want to catch a case messing around with Les and Jovonta. They can take that drama elsewhere because I'm not about that life.

I came to Smith & Jameson International Beer

Garden, my favorite bar, to meet with the guys about Platinum Prestige. It's an elite concierge service my girl Hunter started a little over a year ago. It surprised me when she asked me to join her, Charlee, Harper, Parker, Chase, Jordan, Payton, Alex, and Ryann as an equal partner. But I jumped at the chance to work with my guys. Now, we're working out the kinks before Hunter goes on maternity leave.

I glance across the room, and the waitress is heading my way again. I bounce across the seat to the end of the booth. I drop a tip on the table and move to the bar. She gives a real smile when she sees the twenty. I give a fake smile back after her nice-nasty attitude all evening, but whatever.

I sit at the bar looking ahead at my reflection. My hair is in two-strand twists pulled away from my face with a little mascara, eyeliner, and gloss. No foundation or lipstick. Growing up, my mother kept my hair in elaborate styles, and she worked with professional makeup artists. Now, I keep it simple. Maybe that's why Les keeps putting me through this drama.

"No, it's because he's a no-good dog." I reach for the dispenser, and I fold the scratchy white napkin and dab at my eyes. I won't blame myself. He did this to us.

"Can I get you something, Taylor?" Martinez asks. He's the regular bartender.

"Uh..." I glance around trying to decide, but I can't think straight.

"How about one of these?" The man next to me taps his glass. I look down, and it appears pinkish-red.

"What is it?"

He picks it up, examines it, then he shrugs. "You have to ask him. It's a holiday special and not bad. A little too fruity for me. Join me because I've heard horrible things about people who drink alone." His smile spreads slow, and I feel blessed to witness it. He's handsome with dark brown hair and hazel eyes.

"I'll take one with extra ice," I tell Martinez.

"Ahhhh come on. You can't add extra ice. Add her drink to my tab."

"No, I can—"

"I insist. Besides I want to make a toast." He lays a hand on my arm, and I stare at it. His touch sends a pulse of warmth through my body, and I feel my heartbeat kick up a notch. His shining eyes widen, and the hue of his skin deepens. I glance away because it's obvious he feels it too.

"Thank you." I pull my arm away and twiddle my thumbs wondering, *What the hell was that?* I clear my throat and reach for the drink placed in front of me. I tip the glass and let a slash pass my lips. It's delicious. I taste a hint of rum and some sort of juice. I turn to the generous stranger. "What are we toasting to?"

"My father." His voice is low and gruff. "Let's see..." He holds up a shot glass and I see the hint of tears lingering in his eyes. "To the man, I never knew. He gave me everything and nothing. He served his country with honor and... huh. Happy Memorial Day."

He touches his glass to mine, throwing back his drink. I watch taking a sip of mine, realizing I'm not the only one having a rough night. I'm not the best person to offer advice, but I feel compelled to ask.

"Want to talk about it?"

"It's simple, really. My father died shortly after my birth. He was a Marine. So, he gave me everything...life, wealth, liberty."

"And the nothing part?"

"He didn't raise me. So, I can't recall his laugh, his advice, nothing. So, he didn't give me any of the things I needed to mature into the man I am today."

"I guess that makes sense."

He laughs, but I hear no humor. "If you understand that, you're worse off than I am. Your turn, gorgeous."

My eyes snap to his. He's a stranger. I guess I could tell him because I'm too embarrassed to tell the guys. So, I take a deep breath. "I found out my ex-fiancé got his baby's mother pregnant."

"Damn." He whistles. "Martinez, refill for the lady."

"Yeah, that pretty much sums it up." I feel an odd sense of relief saying the words as if it makes it all a hardcore fact. I take the new glass, this time, I can identify the flavors of the rum and pineapple. Yeah, that's what that citrus taste is. I turn to...whatever his name is. "What's your name?"

"Zachary Russell." He extends a hand in my direction. I hesitate not wanting to touch him again. But I'm not rude.

"Taylor Wallace." I shake his hand, and instead of pulling away, I hold it for a few extra seconds before placing my hand back in my lap.

We drink in silence. I turn on the barstool towards the lounge across the room glad there's live music tonight from Isaac Jones and his band. They were a regular act here before signing with Star Status Entertainment.

"How are you planning to handle your fiancé?"

"My ex-fiancé." I glance over and back at the stage. Isaac has a fantastic voice. It goes down smooth like this drink. "I'm not doing anything with him. I told him I wanted him out before I get home."

"Bravo." He holds up a hand and slaps me a high-five, and I laugh. He smiles again, and I can't breathe, and a wicked idea washes over me.

He places his glass on the bar giving me his attention. I'm entranced by the feline gold quality of his eyes. There's something about his barely-there beard that makes Zachary sexy, and he just might be what I need to scrub Les' infidelity out of my mind.

"You know what they say about getting over someone."

"Where is that one going?" He smiles.

I totally blame my bestie Charlee. She has the

weirdest sayings and tonight I'm using it because I don't want to think about Les or about going home to an empty house or about knowing he slept with her and got her pregnant again and... "Zachary, would you like to get out of here?"

One eyebrow lifts and I can't believe the words came out of my mouth.

"A responsible man would say no. You're hurt right now. You may see the situation differently after you sleep on it. Because it could all be a misunderstanding."

"Are you a responsible man?"

I lean forward trying my best to flirt. I move close enough to see the flecks of yellow in his eyes, and the scent of his cologne surrounds me. I've never really had to flirt. Les was my first and only. But now I'm a single woman fighting to forget.

"I am a responsible man. But you're asking me after a few drinks. I think it's a crime to seduce an emotionally vulnerable man."

I throw my head back, laughing. "Emotionally vulnerable?"

He nods, leaning closer. "Yes. I told you about my father, and it's Memorial Day."

"Should I take my offer back?" I glance up, his gaze holds me captive, and I want to experience the desire I see directed at me.

"And shatter my excitement?" He holds a hand over his heart.

"Excitement?" I'm smiling again, and the sensation becomes a demanding pulse of need.

"A beautiful woman asking to spend time with an emotional wreck like myself." He shrugs. The joke is barely off his lips before I kiss him.

The taste of the too fruity drink passes between us. His thin lips sandwich mine, then he tilts his head, and I want more. I slip my tongue in his mouth, and Zachary pulls me to him. This kiss is deep, slow, and daring as our heads are moving back and forth to get the absolute best angle to taste perfection.

My heart hammers in my chest as he kisses down my jaw to my neck. This too is new. It is hot and heavy and happening in the bar. Then suddenly he pulls away. We're breathing heavy, our chests rise and fall. I want more.

"Taylor, I'd love to take you back to my place. But I don't want you to wake up and regret your decision."

"I'm not asking for forever. I want a night of amazing sex. To feel hot and fulfilled and to maybe drown out knowing my ex-fiancé had two kids with another woman while in a relationship with me." I stutter out the words. Les' betrayal hurts, and I want to make the ache go away.

"Is he here?" He scans the room, his eyes blaze with anger.

Desire masks the broken places in me where trust used to live, and I want Zachary even if it's only for one night.

"No." I plant my feet on the floor. I wiggle closer to him because I know he wants me as much as I want him.

"Let's bounce."

"*My* car or yours?" I can't believe I'm taking Taylor to my place. I should explain it's been closed for a couple of years. But right now, talking seems like a waste of time.

"Yours. What's your address?"

I tell her opening the car door. She pulls out her cellphone and is sending a text message as I close her inside. I climb in settling behind the steering wheel.

Music fills the car. I glance over, and a smile crosses her face.

I turn over the engine, and my car purrs to life. The new leather smell and a hint of Taylor's perfume fills my nose.

The volume of the song is high, I reach for the knob, and she stops me. I leave it and let the base boom through our bodies as the city flies past us.

I went to the bar to drink my blues away. I wonder

if it will always hurt. It could be my recent discharge from the Marines, or maybe it was losing my mother, either way, the ache seems more real than ever.

I went to the Marines to share something with my father, and now I understand. The military made a man of me. But I walked away last week a fraction of the man I was before I entered.

Repeat tours in Afghanistan changed me.

"I haven't fully unpacked." I pull up in my driveway and into the garage.

"This is a new place?"

"No, I've had it for a while but used it as a rental until I was discharged." She reaches to open the door. "I'll get it."

I circle the car and let her out. I like the way she feels in my arms.

"Are you from here?" Her curious eyes look up into mine.

"I was born here and raised in Kansas. My mother's family lives there. My father's family is from Texas."

"That's why you're here?"

"No, I'm here working on a business contract."

I open the door and let her inside. The house is more house than I'll ever need. But it was one of the properties left by my father.

I drop my keys on the counter. "Would you like something to drink?"

"No, thank you."

She's looking around. This may happen, and it may

not, either way, I'm thankful for Taylor. I would have sat at that bar drinking alone, at least now I have someone to talk to.

"Let's sit in the family room."

She pauses, looking at my paintings on the walls. She studies each not rushing, and I study her. Her skin is lighter than peanut butter, she's average height, toned body, with a nice ass. She looks back at me as if reading my thoughts.

Her face is a perfect oval with lips that are soft as pillows. She had on gloss until I kissed her, and I want to kiss her again. But I call on my military training to remain in my seat.

She's been hurt enough for tonight. I'll enjoy her company then take her back to her car.

"Wait…they're yours?" She points.

I nod.

"You're extremely talented." She steps closer, examining my signature in the right corner.

"Thank you. It's something I learned to embrace in therapy, and it stuck."

"Therapy?"

My chest tightens as I search her face for judgment or fear, and I see neither.

"I was a soldier." That's the best answer I can give. I stand feeling self-conscious. That's not why I brought her here. "I bet you think this is the worst one-night stand ever."

"No, I'm thinking the exact opposite." She walks

over to me. "Thank you for serving our country, and I'm sorry for your loss." She raises to her tiptoes and kisses me. Not like at the bar. This is soft as a caress.

I circle my hands around her neck, holding her mouth to mine. She wraps her hands around my wrists, and I explore her mouth. Her lips are my playground, and she moans, encouraging me to continue. I didn't expect to have a beautiful woman like her with me tonight. I release her sliding my hands around her body. I could kiss her forever.

I feel her hands hook around my waistband. There's a tug on my shirt before her hands feather inside. I gasp, staring down into her eyes. The hunger I see makes me believe for a moment she could be mine. A trail of heat follows her as she grips my butt. She moans again, and it vibrates through my chest.

"You have a nice butt." Her lips brush against mine as she speaks.

"Thank you." I chuckle returning the favor. I tug on the dress bringing the hem up to her waist. I tremble with anticipation the moment I feel her skin beneath my fingers. I step back looking behind her. I kneel and bite at her ass, and she swats at me. "Don't be selfish. You have plenty to share."

And I mean it. I want to take her upstairs to my bedroom. But not without clearing the air. I stand and place a finger under her chin, bringing her eyes to mine.

"Are you sure about this?" I want to remind her

that relationships take more than one night to end. I know. I was married and divorced. It took years to get that woman out of my system. She was like a toxic poison.

"I am."

"One-night stands aren't usually like this." I joke, and I'm surprised by her wide-eyed expression. A thought whispers through my head, she's never done this before. "Taylor, have you done this before?" I bounce my finger between us.

"What? A white guy?" Her mischievous smile earns her a quick kiss. "Yes."

"That's good to know, I guess. But no, a one-night stand?"

Her head drops and I lift her face with my hand bringing her beautiful dark brown eyes back to mine. The shake of her head is subtle. I would have missed it had I blinked.

"No?" I confirm, and the pressure of her response is real. I have to decide quickly on how to proceed.

"No." The next question is on the tip of my tongue. Then she adds, "I've only had one sexual partner."

I step back. She moves forwards. I give her a stern look.

"Zachary."

"Zach." I smile despite knowing this can't happen tonight. It can't. Why would a man turn this woman away? To cheat not once, but twice.

"Zach, I know this is not normal, and I wouldn't

blame you for changing your mind. But I hope you won't. I feel like I have to do this to move on."

"You're not playing fair here, Taylor."

"Because we're talking too much." Her sexy smile makes my heart warm, and I remind it this is only for one night.

Men like me don't get women like her. She's fated to a man deserving of her, and I know that's not me. And for a brief moment, I think about taking Taylor back to her car. Then she grabs the hem of her dress, lifting it over her head. Her orange laced bra is paired with matching panties.

I drop my head back, squeezing my eyes closed. But I can't scrub the sight of her perfection from my mind. Her hands crawl under my shirt and up my chest. Then I feel her tongue swirl around my nipple. She tosses my shirt across the room with a feminine flick of her wrist, then she unzips my pants with a flirty twist of her hips, dropping it like it's hot. She stops hovering over my cock before standing, and it's over.

I gather her in my arms, and her legs wrap around my waist. Her mouth covers mine. The urgent thrust of her tongue matched by the arching of her back. I walk up the stairs lowering her to my bed. I hover over her letting my eyes feast on her beauty. If I can only have her once, I want all of her. I seal the deal with a kiss.

I kneel starting at her toes and kissing up her legs. I smell honey on her skin as I nip and sample my way up. I bite the inside of her thigh, sending her legs open.

I lick my lips, ready to taste heaven, and she scoots back up the bed.

"Taylor, is there something else I should know?" She crosses her hands over her patch of pleasure.

"I've never done that."

"That what?" This woman is something else. I crawl on the bed following.

"You know what I'm talking about and don't laugh." The last part sounds like a whine. I grip her thighs loving the firm thickness in my hands. I slide her from the headboard.

"This is part of a one-night stand," I say matter-of-factly. Who knew I'd have this much fun tonight?

"Noooo…"

I nod.

"You do that," she wags her finger toward her southern region, "to every woman?"

I can't help but laugh. "Sorry, baby, no. Not at all."

"Good."

"But I will with you." I lick my lips ready because I know it will be unforgettable like her.

"You will?"

I nod, scooting her until she's flat on her back. "And, Taylor, you'll love it."

"Love is a strong word. Not sure I'm a fan of it. Which is neither here nor there."

Her eyes dance with nervousness, but it will fade soon. It could be selfish, but the joy of knowing I'll share this first with her makes me eager. Tonight, she'll see what she's been missing.

"It's a strong and accurate word. Now, stop talking."

ZACH SLITHERS DOWN MY BODY, and I look up at the ceiling. A bubble of anticipation circles in my stomach. The guys have mentioned it in passing. I was too unsure to ask questions. I chalked it up to dating and having sex with Les as a teenager. We pretty much stick to missionary. Every once in a while, we had sex on the couch. But that's basically the extent of my sexual knowledge.

He's between my legs kissing down my stomach. I tense when his tongue dips into my belly button.

"Zach…"

His head comes up. "Yes, baby?"

"This makes me so nervous." The words stumble out, and I take a deep breath as waves of anxiety rush through my body.

"We'll try, and if you're still nervous, I'll stop."

I can't imagine him stopping, but his patience makes me relax. I run my hand through his hair.

"Are you regretting this?" I ask.

"I think you've changed my Memorial Day blues for good."

"Really?"

"Really. Thank you." He sits up and kisses me. "Enough talking."

I stare up wondering what the heck have I agreed to. But I've always been curious. Then I feel his tongue sweep across my clit. I gasp clinching my legs. He grips my thighs with his hands, lowering my heat onto his long thick tongue.

I grab a handful of his hair. His mouth works me, and I can't believe I've never done this. He picks up the pace as my butt lifts from the mattress. I feel release within my grasp, and he's doing it with his mouth.

Then he thrusts and sucks, and I scream his name. He pulls back with the look of raw maleness, slipping a condom over his manhood. I look at his package. He lays back and tells me to come to him. I gladly follow his lead.

"Ride me, baby."

I pause, this is a night of newness for me. I can't stop to think about how I'll feel in the morning, or about what's next. His knowing eyes search mine.

"Straddle my body." His command sends heat flowing through my veins like lava as he pats the mattress on either side of him.

I obey.

"Lean towards me, and I'll help you."

I bring my chest to him, and he grips my hips. I kiss him tasting myself on his mouth, and I thank him with my heart for his patience.

"Ready…"

I place my hands on his shoulders. He thrusts, filling me. We groan in unison.

"Zach…" He's big and fills me from wall to wall.

"Sit into it."

I sit back, rocking my hips. I get lost in the rhythm of his caressing, his words. It hurts so good. And for the second time tonight I feel release calling my name. The thought of him doing this with another causes my eyes to fly open, and I see pleasure written across his handsome face.

"Oh shit…I gotta fill you, baby."

He flips me on my back, and the strokes are deep. His hips slamming into mine. This is death of the best kind. Then he pulls out and plunges deep once more, a chorus of our cries fill the air. The pleasure is pure and explosive.

I pass out immediately.

CHAPTER 3

TAYLOR

I have a meeting in less than ten minutes, and there's no way I'm making it on time. Last night was... I can't find the words. My body is still quivering from it all. Zach loved my body from top to bottom and back again until I left. I showered and changed into some borrowed clothes. He dropped me off, and I wonder if we'll see each other again.

Is that what I want?

The fact that I haven't thought about Les is telling. He could have stayed at my house for all I know. I'll deal with it later.

I'm back at S&J. It's before business hours. I wave at Martinez as I head back to the conference room, the moment I enter the conversations stop.

This is pretty much our office. The owners let us use the space since Ben, Hunter's husband, was a manager here until he started working for Platinum Prestige.

The fact that I look like a bum is not missed by anyone in attendance. Hunter is talking, but all eyes are on me. I feel exposed like they all know what I did last night.

I take a vacant chair next to Parker. I'm still having an out of body moment because I've been thoroughly sexed and I know they know. Parker hands me the agenda. I read it to avoid the questioning stares.

I would have skipped the meeting, but I have to go over the database I'm building. Hunter hits her stride, and I focus on the timeline. Every guy has her head down, taking notes. We're growing at a slow and steady pace, to date, we've signed a dozen clients.

Ben takes over adding in details about the balance of the workload while Hunter is on maternity leave having the twins.

Most of us met in high school bonding over the fact that we have guy names. Hence the "guys." This business venture has sealed our bond as friends and sisters.

Hunter, Charlee, and Harper are the OGs of the group. They've known each other the longest. I met the others through Charlee, so I naturally gravitate towards her. I honestly float between the internal clusters, hanging with pretty much all of them. But Parker, Jordan and I live in the same subdivision, so we hang out several times a week.

The meeting shifts, and each guy gives a quick update about their assignment. I take notes. I'm building a database to house our contacts, services, and incoming leads, which means I'm using the skills I acquired in college. Jordan is building a custom app. She and I are planning to have coffee later at my place to compare notes.

The others are focusing on products and services. Harper is working on getting a lease for a private plane, and Parker is scouting office space.

Hunter calls for a break, but no one moves. I glance up from my notes to find nine pairs of eyes on me. Ben excuses himself. I watch him go, and I glance back at them, as my heart drums in my ears.

Might as well get it over with. "I had a one-night stand." I blurt it out and wait for the wave of responses. But no one says a word.

I'm surprised.

When I need it said like it is…or the untamed god-honest truth, there's one guy to talk to…Charlee. So, I look at her, our resident mouthpiece.

"I'm utterly confused. How can you have a one-night stand with your man?" Her forehead scrunches.

"I told Les to move out." I hear the wave of responses I expected before. Questions, high fives, the constant chatter between them keeps me from having to respond to their glee. It kind of hurts. None of them liked Les, but it wasn't their choice but mine.

Harper changes chairs, moving closer to me. "Honey, what happened?"

Harper is the soul of us. Keeps us honest. I'm usually our assessor of the risk factors, protecting my guys like a mamma would shield of her beloved cubs.

"Jovonta came by to tell me she's pregnant again."

I'm sure I could hear a pin hit the floor. I glance down at my hands. I have nothing to be ashamed of. I didn't cheat. But after last night it makes me wonder if that is why he went elsewhere.

I can't stop my thoughts from seeing Zach between my thighs, Zach inside me, Zach screaming my name. No, if I had to endure Jovonta to have Zach, so be it.

"So, you find out Les cheated again, and you're smiling?" Charlee smiles that wicked one when she's about to turn up. "Aaaahhhhh *shit*! You did the nasty!"

Charlee hops to her feet doing some crazy woman dance twerking and the guys are laughing like hyenas. I join in and find myself huddled in a group hug. I lean in accepting their love and support.

"Can you please tell us? Did he—"

"Charlee!" the guys say in unison.

"Y'all ain't right. Let this girl go her whole entire life without a little licky-licky."

Heat floods my face. I duck my head to keep them from seeing my cheeks turn red. "Y'all are wrong for not insisting," I confirm.

"Oh, dayum!"

We laugh and sit back at the table. I can't tell the

guys everything since I haven't processed it all. So, I share enough to get a little breathing room.

"I met him here last night." I keep Zach's name to myself. No point in being specific since we didn't exchange numbers.

"Did he ask or you?"

"I did." The collective head whip causes a gush of air to move through the room. "We shared a couple of drinks, and I told him about Les and his baby mama drama. Then I asked him to take me home."

"Then what?" Charlee asks.

"Y'all know."

"No, we don't," Parker says, leaning forward on her knees.

"We basically did stuff." I giggle. "Dang. Just know I had a different experience." I shrug and wait for the next question.

"So, you're done with Les?"

"Yes."

The room falls deathly silent. I've been here before, we've been here before. Not the one-night stand but the Les fucking up part. Then he has a way to wiggle past my defenses. The number one reason is always saving the years we've spent working on our relationship. He's one of the oldest relationships in my life. And he was the single piece of hope that I could one day have a normal family.

Husband, wife, and kids.

I tug at the sleeves on Zach's shirt. I hold it up to my

nose, smelling his scent. I smile, wondering what he's doing.

"He got it like that?" Parker asks.

I freeze. Looking at the sleeve near my nose.

"So, you understand the definition of a one-night stand is it's for one...night?" Charlee holds up her index finger.

"Charlee I'm not stupid." I'm offended. But part of me wants a repeat, which means it wouldn't be a one-night stand but two unless we see each other before the day's out. *What is wrong with me?* I'm trying to find a loop hole to a one-night stand.

I fall forward not caring that they're all looking at me. This is awkward and uncomfortable. But I get it. This is what we do. I've just never been the center of attention.

"You want to go back for more." Jordan reads me.

"Okay. So, it was amazing." I groan. "I mean amazing *amazing*. And no! Charlee I won't tell you the nasty details because they are nasty. Like the good kind that will have me thinking about—" I stop, covering my face with my hands.

"Hot dayum!"

I don't know who said it because they're all squealing around me like the cheerleaders of my life. This is the best part of our friendship. The guys are down when I'm right or wrong. They question me, but I know this is a soft place for me to land.

"Taylor!"

I turn, and Les is standing in the doorway. Ben and Asher are standing over his shoulder.

"What do you want? I'm in the middle of a meeting."

He glances between the guys. This was another downfall of our relationship. He hates my guys, but we're a package deal. He mumbles his comments under his breath and it's another strike against him.

"We need to talk," Les says.

"Speak your piece." I cross my arms.

"Alone."

"Talk now or leave. They stay, or you can leave." I can see Parker and Jordan from my peripheral vision. I want to turn and hug them all. But first, I need to get rid of him.

"I can explain," he says.

"Oh, this should be good." I hear from behind me.

He snarls at someone over my shoulder.

"I'm waiting."

"I was dropping off Vonnie and—"

"Please tell me you're not going to give another sloppy ass excuse." Harper stops the ridiculous response in its tracks.

I turn to Harper, and I smile. My girl is coming out of her shell. Must be Liam's influence.

"Save the bullshit. Les this is the second time you've done this. It's over. We're over."

"We can get past this Taylor. We can't just throw over ten years like that."

"Apparently that's not true, because you did it, not

once but twice. Les, I loved you. And at some point, I have to draw the line. This is it." I draw a line in the air. This has nothing to do with Zach and everything to do with Les. I allowed this behavior to continue, and now I'm reaping the consequences.

"Loved?" He reaches for me, and I step back.

"Did you move your things?" I ask.

"No, because we need to talk about this."

"We just did, and I want you out by noon. Goodbye, Les."

He opens his mouth to respond, and Ben steps inside the room, telling him it's time to leave. I brush away the tears running down my cheeks. I'm not sad. Maybe it will hit me later when I get home. Right now, I embrace the relief of knowing I'm moving on.

I feel an arm wrap around my shoulders. I lean my head on Parker's shoulder. "Proud of you."

"Me too." Harper rubs my back.

"Want us to head over to your place?" Hunter asks.

"No, you guys have helped enough. I need to do this part alone." I turn to face them. "I need to close this chapter."

They nod, and I hug each one accepting their words of encouragement. Hunter closes out the meeting. I have notes to review on the database. But my only task at this moment is watching the only man I've ever loved to leave my life for good.

CHAPTER 4

ZACH

I can't stop thinking about Taylor. I'm honestly not the one-night stand type. My career as a soldier and now building a technology company left me with no time for anything other than work. But Taylor was…is different. I should have asked for her number.

It's been a few weeks, and I've been by S&J daily hoping to see her again with no luck. I considered asking the bartender since he knew her by name, but I decided against it. She was clear that it was meant to be a one-night stand. An ache fills my chest at this reality. I should have done more. I guess the memories will be all I have of her.

I focus on the document on the screen in front of me. I started a consulting company before leaving the Marines. I type the finishing touches on the proposal

I'm pitching at the end of the week. Work is the best way to move forward.

I work until I can't see the words on the screen. I hear the chime of my phone. I rub my eyes and check my text messages. I smile as I read the text, *I'm in town. Close your laptop and meet me at S.&J.*

I chuckle, *I'll be there in twenty.*

I grab my keys. Darius Grant is one of my closest friends. We met overseas and bonded as Americans traveling abroad. We've stayed in contact while he's built his company. He's the one who told me about S&J.

I walk through my house, zig-zagging through the unpacked boxes. Most of them hold my clothes and the taller ones against the walls are more of my paintings. I glance around. I'm still not sure if I'll stay in Austin or head back to California. But I might as well set up my home.

I lock the door behind me as I get in my car. I try to tell myself my decision to set up my house has nothing to do with Taylor. It's a lie. It wasn't just sex with her. But I'm a firm believer in what is meant to be, will be.

I drive to the warehouse district and park. The music greets me as I walk to the hostess. I hear Darius' boisterous voice and glance up. He pulls me into a brotherly hug patting my back.

"Man, how's it going?" he asks, guiding me to a table.

"When did you get into town?"

"Last night. My lady had a meeting with her

business partners. You want to grab food first?" He points to the courtyard.

"Yeah, I'm starving. I've been working on the last details of my proposal all day." I scan the room with military precision. She's not here. Then I stop at seeing a cluster of beautiful women walking in our direction.

"Did you finish it?" He turns around and smiles at seeing the ladies. "Let me introduce you to my lady." He bends a finger beckoning a woman over from the group.

The grin on his face is one I haven't seen on him before. Curious, I turn to see "his lady." A brown skinned woman steps from the pack. It's as if time stops as she crosses the room, heads turn watching her until she stops in front of Darius. But with all of her beauty, it's the look in her eyes that tell it all. She loves him.

I've never had someone look at me like that. Not even my ex-wife.

"Zach, man, this is my lady, Charlee Raine." His voice drops, and he kisses her neck. Her girly giggle makes me smile too.

"Stop, boy." She slaps at his chest, not pulling away. They quickly kiss then she extends a hand to me. "It's Charlee. Don't listen to this crazy man."

Darius throws back his head and laughs. It's like I'm meeting my friend for the first time. I watch them throw words around like confetti.

"We have a guy SOS." She throws her head a little towards the ladies waiting for her.

"All right. Holler if you need me." He kisses her.

She's good for him. He's always been focused and intense, but this Darius seems relaxed and in love.

"Always." She rubs at the lipstick on his lips. Then turns her sparkling gaze to me. "It was nice meeting you."

"Same to you."

"All right, babe. I'm out."

Darius doesn't stop watching until she disappears. And suddenly I realize I'm ready for a lady, for someone special. I've traveled and lived a full life. I don't have to marry again, but it would be nice to have someone look at me the way Charlee looks at Darius.

"That must be nice."

"What's that?" Darius starts for the courtyard, and I follow.

"Having a lady like that in your life." I look around at the trucks. "Man, you were right about this place. They need to build one in San Francisco."

"Nah, I'd gain a million pounds." He laughs, heading for the barbecue truck. I shrug and go with him. We wait in line. "Charlee and I used to date in college. Then I left to travel and train."

"Were you together?"

He shakes his head. "She wasn't interested in traveling or having a long-distance relationship."

"But you're back together now."

"Yeah, but I had to pull out all the stops. My lady ain't no joke." He laughs. "Man, what you want I got you."

"I'll have whatever you're ordering. I haven't eaten barbecue in years."

"Get ready to have sauce up to your elbows." I laugh covering my mouth because Darius has an understated sense of humor. He keeps me on my toes, and he's a people magnet. A quality I wish I had.

We get our food and sit outside. "How'd you get her back?"

"Man, I had to get my shit together." He stops glancing out over the crowd rubbing his hands on a napkin. "I was a kid when I fell in love with her. But I was broke, didn't have shit. And she had it all."

"That's hard on a man."

"Yeah, but that's her and her guys. So, I had to prove myself. Not for her, but for me."

"I bet you took her on the jet." I glance over.

"Man…" We laugh. "You know I had to flex a little."

I nod. "I'd flex too."

We eat, and I think about Taylor. "I think I met someone."

"Word? And?"

"Nothing really. It was a one-night situation, but she made an impression."

He stops, scanning me. "And you didn't pursue it."

"I didn't, and now I'm hoping I don't regret it."

"Do I know her?"

I shrug. "I don't know, but she was in a situation. So, it could be for the best."

"What about you? I haven't seen you get serious with a woman since Amanda."

"After that, I didn't *want* to get serious about anyone." I push the tray away. Amanda made me lose all faith in love.

"All love ain't like that."

"So, are we talking from experience?" I lean back, teasing him a little.

"No doubt. I've always loved Charlee. I doubt that will ever change. What about you? Are you done being a rich bachelor? I could see if Charlee can hook you up with one of her friends."

"I'm good for now. I'll let you know if that changes." A part of me hopes I'll see Taylor. I'd ask her out and see if we could continue what we started.

"So, tell me about this proposal." He leans forward taking a drink from his cup. "Is it a solo bid?"

We talk about my business proposal for the next hour. Darius has a candy company but a business mind. I get his input about pitching as a small business to a large brand. I'm a coding specialist. The company put out a call for contractors. I got a personal introduction to the CEO from my commanding officer, and now here I am.

"Are you relocating to Austin?" I ask him later as we stand to leave.

"I hope so. But I have so much to clear up at home. So, I expect we'll bounce back and forth since Charlee's company is here and mine is in San Francisco. What about you?"

"I'm open. I'm setting up my place, but this bid will make the final determination. They have locations around the states."

"Well, holler at me when you get back to California."

"You know it." We hug and say our goodbyes.

I watch him leave and turn back to S&J. I'm more confident in my proposal thanks to Darius' input. I head to my car. I have my meeting to present tomorrow. I scan the area once more, just in case, then I drive home enjoying the scenery in Austin.

My thoughts float back to my ex-wife Amanda. Divorce felt like the worst kind of death. It was the death of more than our vows but our friendship too. At the time, Amanda wanted marriage, and I didn't. But I asked because I thought it would make her happy. It did for a while, but eventually, she began to want more. A house. New cars. It was when we approached the topic of kids that our lives went from bad to awful.

She wanted a house full, and I didn't. Having kids with Amanda would have been a leash, and I can't see myself as a father. I wouldn't have the slightest idea where to begin. It was always my mother and I since she never remarried or dated much.

I pull into my garage, killing the engine. Maybe it's best to remain single and build my business. But an inner yearning is not ready to push the thought of Taylor aside.

CHAPTER 5

TAYLOR

J pack a suitcase ready to leave Austin. I toss clothes across the room, moving with haste. Against my better judgment and the advice of my guys, I gave in to Les' requests to hang out as friends. He kept coming by until I folded. He came to me saying Jovonta was lying about the pregnancy. But the fact that there is a possibility that the child is his is reason enough to leave him for good.

Over the summer we had a few dinner outings, and we went to a couple of concerts. I saw a glimpse of the Les I fell in love with, but every time he tried to kiss me, I had thoughts of Zach.

"Are you going to tell me what this is about?" Charlee is on speaker phone.

I stop throwing clothes. "I can't stop thinking about Zach."

"Zach…Zach…"

37

"My one-night stand."

"Ohhh… It was that good." I hear the tone of her voice and roll my eyes.

It was, but I can't tell her that because she'll squeal and dance. "It's not that. He was different," I tell her.

"How much do you think the sex had to do with it?"

"It had something, of course. But we talked and no matter how much I try to push Zach out of my mind, I can't."

"Do you want to?"

I face the phone. "Want to what?"

"Let him go."

I sit on the bed, holding a shirt to my chest. It's crazy to still think about a guy that has probably moved on. I tried chalking it up to the oral sex for the first time, then riding him, another first. I feel a connection that I didn't have with Les, and to me, that's saying a lot. It's a constant yearning that won't let me be.

"You still there?"

"Yes. Charlee, how do you know when it's time to move on?"

"I wish I could tell you. All I can say is trust yourself. Some relationships are only for a season, but we don't know it until we embark on the journey."

"That was deep, Charlee."

She laughs. "Shut up. Real talk. I thought I wasn't ready for Darius. But he came when I needed him. If it had been a minute sooner, or a minute later, who knows what would have been. What about Les?"

"That's over. We'll always have a friendship. But as far as being a couple, I'm done with that chapter of my life. Tell me about San Francisco."

Charlee talks. She moved out there to help Darius. They fly back and forth.

"While you're here I can introduce you to Darius' best friend. Hey, his name is Zach too."

"It's not the name. But whatever. I'm game."

"Whaaaat!" She has an annoying way of singing when she's excited, like now.

"Change the subject crazy lady. I'm excited about my trip."

I'm thankful for their generous invitation to come for a visit. I'm almost done with the Platinum Prestige database, but I need to get away to focus on finishing it. And maybe I'll consider dating again. It's time for a new direction.

My phone beeps and I glance at the display. It's my mother.

"Charlee, I'll call you when I land. Love you, girl!"

"Love you back."

"Hey, Mom. Are you back in LA?" I start folding the clothes and placing them inside my suitcase.

"I am for a few days then I'm heading out to New York to meet with some distributors. How are you?"

"I'm better. I'm packing to visit Charlee in San

Francisco. It would be cool to stop through and see you."

"I'd love to see you, baby. So, catch me up."

We settle in talking. My mother is the closest person to me. I can tell her anything, but she's more like a friend than a mother.

Tyesha Rose Wallace is a black hair care mogul. She's all things hair—weave, styling tools, products, accessories. She started a neighborhood beauty supply store to support us. But she didn't settle for getting her supplies locally, she saved fifty thousand dollars and flew to China. She now supplies other stores across the country through her supply chain.

She's a self-made millionaire and thanks to her efforts I'm free to live as I choose. But her aspirations came at a cost, I missed so much growing up. She jet-setted from coast to coast closing deals, and I stayed at home with a live-in nanny. And all the while I missed my mother and my deadbeat father.

"You're visiting distributors in New York?"

"I am, some of my Chinese suppliers are building stateside distribution centers."

"That's amazing. I bet you'll save time and money."

"Yes, I'll celebrate if I can cut my Beijing trips down to a couple times a year. Did you get your database working?"

"Yes and no. I have the program almost ready to add actual data. But it crashes when I'm trying it import csv or spreadsheet data."

"Does the crash wipe out the data or just kick you out?"

"Unfortunately, both." I smile. My mother has a knack for absorbing information and using it to interact with people. It's a skill I need to learn. "How do you do that, Ma?"

"What, baby?" I can hear the smile in her voice, and I miss her. I hope we get together while I'm in California.

"How do you use what I've told you in a conversation?" I sit again now that my bag is packed.

"Active listening. People usually say a fraction of what they mean. I use it all, body language, context clues, past conversations. All of it gives me a full view of who I'm dealing with."

"I'm going to work on that." I sit up straighter.

"You already are, baby girl. Keep doing what you're doing. And if I haven't told you, I'm proud of you. You guys are doing the damn thing!"

I laugh. "We are. Thank you, Mom, I have an amazing example."

"Do you really believe that?"

"What do you mean? That you're an amazing example?"

"Yes. I always feel a disconnect between us concerning your professional pursuits."

I pause thinking about her statement. "It's hard to tell my strong mother that I have no desire to work full time. I couldn't find a way to say it and not offend you or belittle your accomplishments."

"Why do you fight it?"

"I feel like I missed out on my childhood with you because you traveled building your business. For many years I was jealous, not of your boyfriends but of the business."

"Wow. I didn't know that. What about now?"

"Platinum Prestige is changing my perspective. I see how hard we're working. I'm working on coding daily. I'm testing and revising. I can only imagine how much Hunter is working to prepare for the babies or how the other guys are traveling to make this company succeed."

I stand walking the length of my bedroom. "But, Mom, I appreciate all you've done. Parts of me want to join the family business, but other parts want to live my dream. I want to get married and have a family."

"Baby, you can do both. Yes, I was extreme. But I was building something out of nothing. I'm assuming Les is officially out of the picture."

"Your assumption is right. I had another encounter with his daughter's mother."

"That boy must think I'm playing. I don't play about my only child." I hear her moving around on the other end.

"Mom, I'm okay. I see the relationship for what it is. I spent too much time hoping and praying for him to change. It is time for me to do the changing."

"Who brought this on?"

"A friend." I smile.

"Do I know this friend? Because whoever he is, I owe him a drink." She laughs.

"You don't know him, and I'll pass the message." I see Zach's face, and my body tingles with awareness. I'm going to find him. I have his full name and with Facebook, Google, and friends. Someone must know him.

"I'll let you get for your flight. I'll make sure I'm around. I can always fly up to San Francisco. I haven't seen Charlee Raine in years. How long will you be there?"

"I'm thinking a week or so. I'll work out there. Darius, her boyfriend, wants to meet with me about building a similar database for his company."

"See, Taylor, this is the best of both worlds. You have friends and options. I had no connections, no money, no guys. Now you can see how staying with your guys or coming this way is truly possible. I just want you happy."

My eyes water. "I love you."

"I love you more. You're my heart, Taylor. I'm looking forward to seeing how your life evolves. Because I think you can have it all."

I think I can too. I have to keep pushing and trusting myself. I hang up the phone, ready to leave for the airport and to find Zach.

CHAPTER 6

ZACH

The smell of rich coffee beans surrounds me the moment I step foot into the small cafe. The contrast between the light wood floors and the cherry red walls clash as much as it blends. I went over to Darius' place, but he and Charlee are stuck in a meeting. He suggested this place since it's up the hill from their place.

I figure I'll work until they call me. So, I walked the short distance, and now I'm looking for a place to work near a power outlet. The middle of the cafe has long-running light wood tables with power strips and tulips running between them.

The small round tables lining the perimeter are more appealing because I can work alone. I see an empty table near the window. I walk over, dropping my bag and go to the counter to order my coffee.

I moved from Austin after accepting the contract

with Tech Secure. They needed my presence at their headquarters here in San Francisco. Thankfully I still have my house. I order my black drip coffee squeezing through the chairs and tables. I sit and take a drink of the blonde roast, taking a moment to appreciate the oversized bay window.

The transition has been difficult. The facility manager wasn't too keen on having an outside programmer working on the program extension. But the CEO wanted my expertise with high-level security, and when I complete this project, he foresees more in the future.

I open my laptop and dig in. I reach for my headphones to drown out the sounds of people talking, a crying baby, and the espresso machine when I hear a familiar sound. The hairs on my neck stand. My eyes sweep the room from the right to the left, slowly turning my body until I see her.

My chest tightens. The woman who's haunted my dreams for six months is across the room. The sound was a moan. She's holding a to-go coffee cup with two hands. She brings the cup to her mouth, and her eyes lock with mine.

A sense of relief fills my body. I lost something important, and it's not until this moment that my brain and heart stand in unity…*it's Taylor*.

I missed her. I wanted her. But I wondered if I'd ever find *her*.

She lowers the cup, and I see the tremble of her

hands. I grab my bag, not wasting time. I cross the room. The moment I reach the table, she stands, and I fold her into my arms.

Holding her is filling all the broken places in my soul, and I have no right. She could be back with her fiancé. She could have a new man in her life. Yet I hold her tight.

I drop my mouth to her ear.

"I missed the hell out of you."

"I missed you too."

I pull back and see the tears gathering in her eyes. It's insane to think I missed her this much, but the void is apparent at this moment. I've been running from thing to thing, assignment to assignment when all I wanted was Taylor.

I lower to the chair and place her on my lap. She doesn't hesitate to wiggle getting comfortable.

"How are you?" I ask, and she gathers my face in her hands, staring into my eyes. This is where she belongs.

"Better now." I kiss her. And I want to touch her, to make sure it's not another dream. I hold her waist, rubbing my thumbs on her bare stomach. She drops her hands over my shoulders, resting her breast against my chest.

"So much has happened. Business is growing. My database is working, but I'm having issues with it crashing." Her head drops to the side, causing her dreadlocks to cascade around me.

"Mind if I take a look at it?" She smiles, showing her

perfect teeth, but her mouth is my favorite. I kiss her again.

"You program?"

"Yes." I smile, brushing my lips along her upper arm. She's in a sleeveless crop top that makes me think of the matching underwear she wore the last time we were together. "Is orange your favorite color?"

"Yes, how'd you know?"

"A guess." I reach for my coffee to keep from running my hands over her toned body. "I program mostly firewalls and security features, but I'm well versed in Javascript, Python, Java, Php, and others."

"Why didn't I know this?"

"We talked but never about our careers." I push a lock of hair over her shoulder. My eyes hold hers. "I'd like to change that."

"I would too." She leans closer.

"And your ex?"

"He's no longer in the picture."

I'm smiling, and I want to take her back to my place. But I want to get to know her. "Can I have your number?"

Her eyes round and her laughter spills over into my barren soul. The place I've never allowed another person because it's murky. Not even my ex-wife ventured to the depths of me. Is that why it didn't work out? Why she felt the need to seek pleasure from other men?

"Where'd you go just now?"

I caress her soft cheek, thankful for my ex's indiscretions because that's what landed me here with Taylor.

"I thought about you every day for six months. I want you more than I've ever wanted a woman in my life. I just don't want to mess this up. I'm…complicated but I've decided…"

"What did you decide, Zach?"

"That choosing you means I have to open up to you. This might not be the time or the place. But I can't assume I'll get the chance again. Are you down with that?"

"I am, but first I have to tell you something." Her voice falls with her eyes. The subtle shake of her sweet body raises my senses.

"What is it?" I lift her chin wanting to see her beautiful eyes.

"I can't have kids." Her eyes go back to her hands fidgeting in her lap.

"Okay."

"Okay?" She looks up obviously annoyed by my response. "Zach, I'm serious. I can't enter another relationship without placing it out there for us to discuss." She stands, and I place her back where she belongs. "Zach." Her soft plea makes me smile.

"We'll discuss whatever you want, but from right here."

"Fine."

I'm learning a lot about my woman. And yes, she's

mine. I know it with everything in me. I was trained by the best, the United States Marine Corp, to know my opponents, to size them up and take them down. And Taylor doesn't know it, but I'm taking her and all of her walls down.

"Taylor, I'll do whatever I have to do to have you."

Her eyes snap to mine. The unshed tears in her eyes make my heart throb with a need to ensure she never sheds another tear from pain.

"Even this?" She tries to look away.

"I want you. Kids, no kids. Crazy ex. Crazy folks. Crazy friends."

"I think your hormones are talking. Because don't nobody want to deal with a crazy ex." She laughs, kissing the side of my hand. "And my friends are not crazy."

I feel a goofy smile spread across my face. "I've dealt with the worst, and none of it compares to the possibility of having you."

"You can't keep saying stuff like that."

"Why?" Her smile is everything right now.

"Because…" she whispers.

"Because of what?" I'll let her shrug go because I still see the doubt in her eyes. "I'm okay with it because I want you and because I've never wanted children." Her eyes round. "Don't look at me like that."

"Sorry, I've just never heard a man say that."

"I grew up without my father, and my plans were always to be a career Marine. I never wanted a child to experience what I lived through. It's hard growing up as a man without a father. Thankfully, I had many mentors and men around me, growing up. But no one replaces a father."

"I know…it's a hollow void." She kisses me, and the room disappears. "My mother raised me alone, too, except my father isn't dead. He just didn't want me."

"What?"

"Yeah. He paid child support every month. He set up my college fund, and I'm financially secure for the rest of my life. But I never had him." She shrugs. "It is what it is. He is where he is, and I am where I am. I've moved on."

The pain in her eyes makes me want to find the man. I don't believe she's moved on. But this is not the place to explore it further.

"He's missing out on the best part of life, Taylor. That's his bad. But I just want to know one thing." I kiss her neck, letting the smell of her perfume surround me.

"What's that, Zach?"

"Can I be your boyfriend…your boo…your main squeeze…your old man?" She's laughing as I kiss her between each request. I can't believe this woman has me ready to make love to her in the middle of a cafe. But I do, and I want her to always be happy. I want to be the one that makes her happy.

"Yes, Zach…yes to all of it."

She wraps her arms back around my neck. I'm in a

cocoon of Taylor. We kiss. Her hands in my hair, running across my scalp. I drink her in, and my heart sends gratitude to the universe for creating this woman.

I reluctantly end the kiss and hold up my phone. Her laugh makes me laugh. And all is well with my soul. "Now let me see this program before I jump your bones."

I swat her butt, and she stands taking her chair. I sense that we've just crossed a significant hurdle. I got my lady, and all is well with me.

She turns the laptop in my direction. For the next couple of hours, we work side-by-side. Her coding is brilliant and intuitive. I find the code causing the crash. She walks me through her design, and I ask a series of questions. I think this would be a fantastic program for Darius to consider.

"I have a friend with a business in town. He runs a factory. I think this program will help him manage his vendors and clients. I'd love to refer you."

"I'd like that. I've never considered taking on more clients. But I'm planning to hang around for a couple of weeks."

"Really? What brings you to town?"

"I'm visiting my best friend and her boyfriend, which makes me think." She glances at her watch. "I need to get running. They're having a little gathering tonight."

I don't want to leave her side after waiting for half a year.

"Stop giving me that look." She leans over and kisses me. "What to join us?"

"Sure. I need to text Darius." I open my text app not waiting for Taylor to change her mind.

"Darius?"

"Yes, he's my boy. I'm supposed to stop by his place. But I can reschedule."

"Darius Grant?" she says with her head cocked to the side.

"You know him?"

The quiver of her lips tells me she's holding back a laugh. "I'm staying at his place."

"What!" I sit straight up.

"Not like that. Charlee is one of my best friends."

"You're kidding?"

She laughs, falling forward on the table. "So, you're the Zach they're planning to introduce me to tonight?"

"I knew nothing about that. You're dating?"

"No, they were hoping to get me out of my funk." She stands up and comes around the table. She lowers back to my lap. I like the way her fingers brush the sides of my neck.

"You were in a funk? Over the breakup?" Knowing my Taylor still holds feelings for another dude doesn't settle well.

"Yes and no. I was in a funk. It wasn't over the

breakup but over losing touch with an exceptional guy."

The heat in her eyes for someone else has me seeing stars. "I appreciate your honesty, but I can't handle you talking about another dude in my face."

"I wouldn't dare."

I'm confused. I glance off waiting to hear about this guy. Jealousy isn't a natural response for me, but I have a growing suspicion that it's the feeling causing my heart to race, that and the beautiful woman in my lap.

I have no right to be jealous of another man. It's been six months, and we shared a single night together. One. And she has me so open I'm ready to kill the dude.

Her lingering silence causes me to glance up, and I see a sneaky smile.

"I'm waiting." I look out the bay window across the room internally counting.

"Zach, I'm talking about you, silly."

My head snaps in her direction. "What?"

"I realized too late that we didn't exchange phone numbers."

"And I wanted to respect your request to keep it to one night. What changed your mind?" I kiss her pleased with her response.

"I'm not sure I'm ready to share, but I've already told you my sad sappy story." She dips her head, a trait I notice when she's embarrassed.

"Tell me, baby."

"You changed my mind. I had a night of firsts. But it wasn't that. I felt something with you I've never felt before, and I didn't want to go backward."

My chest swells, knowing I made an impression. "We can continue this conversation in private. There's a park up the street. Let's walk and talk."

I selfishly want time alone with her before I share her with the others. She stands, and we gather our belongings. I send Darius a text, and she texts Charlee.

I'm ready to know more about this woman because I have no intentions of letting her go.

CHAPTER 7

"Zach and Darius are best friends." I shake my head. "What are the chances?"

"It's crazy. Pass me that platter." Charlee points to the cabinet behind me.

This kitchen is a cook's dream. The beautiful marble countertops with black appliances. I turn around and see a clear glass serving dish. I place it on the counter. Together we load it with appetizers. I handle the veggies, and she's plating the warm finger foods. I can't miss the chance to tease Charlee.

"I don't think I've ever seen you this domesticated." We laugh.

"Get a good eyeful. Because that fine man can have me pregnant and barefoot in this place and I'd say…yes, sir."

I throw my head back. She finds a way to bring life

to every situation, even make side dishes for dinner under the stars. I steal a baby carrot from her perfect platter. "What do you think about Zach?"

"He seems like a cool dude." She sobers, leaning against the counter. "What do you think?"

"It's like we've known each forever and it's exciting. I'm starting something new after suffocating in something old." The words flow out, and I exhale. Wow…that's precisely how I feel. It's a new beginning. I pop the rest of the carrot in my mouth and look over at her.

Charlee glances over her shoulder at the guys grilling outside before moving closer. She grabs my hands. "I need you to do something for me, Tae."

"Sure."

"I can't ask you not to rush into this. Hell, I moved in with Darius after less than a month of dating again. But please pace yourself. You were in a relationship with Les for your entire adult life. Take your time with Zach."

I swallow, I didn't expect this. "I've waited for months to find him."

"I know, sweetie. No one wants you happy more than me. Just pace yourself."

"I hear you, Charlee," I whisper. She squeezes my hands, and we return to prepping the food.

My mind races through a lifetime of thoughts, hurts, successes, failures. My father, my mother, Les, my guys, and the one common thread is I've never felt as happy as I do right now.

Zach's words flutter to mind, "...none of it compares to the possibility of having you."

I can't say Zach completes me. But I can say he presents an opportunity to experience something new, something real. Especially after telling him, I can't have kids. Maybe for once I can accept that giving birth is not in my plans but enjoying this season in my life with Zach is. Even if it's only for pleasure.

I look over at my best friend, she's preparing steamed vegetables and Jasmine rice. I think about her words and where she's coming from.

"Tae, I joke and clown around, but I want you happy. You've spent years fighting for a man who never seemed as invested as you were." She taps the spoon on the rim of the pot coming across the kitchen, standing beside me at the island.

"I know. But I don't like hearing you say it."

Charlee is not the pump your brakes kind of woman. She's kick off your heels and throw caution to the wind. So, hearing her feelings hurt.

Hunter found Ben. Harper found Liam. Charlee found Darius. I want to find someone too. I glance over her shoulder, and my eyes land on Zach.

"I want you to find a real one. That's all," she adds.

"I think I have..." He waves and I wave back. The corners of his eyes soften, and I decide to follow his lead. I'm choosing him, just as he's decided to choose me.

"Fine. Keep making goo-goo eyes at him like I'm not talking." I kiss her cheek with a loud, smacking sound. "Save your nasty kisses for your man. But know this, if the shit hits the fan, I'll be the first guy swinging." She lowers into her fighter stance with her little fists up.

"Girl, you're a nut!" We laugh and hug. Charlee is our wild child. However, she's the guy you want to ride with you. "I'll be careful. I'm not getting lost in another man. But I'm ready to experience life with him."

"Ain't nothing wrong with that. He's definitely an upgrade." I bump her with my hip. And she rolls her eyes.

"Say I'm lying? I never knew what you saw in Les. But to each her own." She flicks a dismissive hand.

"Hush. Get the food before it gets cold." I get her moving because she'll start in on Les and it's not the point. Not anymore. This is a new day, a new chance at love.

"Whatever! Get the sweet tea."

We carry the food out as they remove the grilled salmon. We grab plates, and Darius blesses the food then we dig in.

It's a beautiful night.

The patio table is rectangular. Zach and I sit on one side, Charlee and Darius on the other. I glance over my shoulder at Zach, and he reaches for my hand under the table. His hands are big and strong. He cups my hip and slides me closer. I lean into him, enjoying the animated conversation going on between Charlee and Darius.

Charlee's hands are flying around. The moment Zach's fingers feather up my thigh, I can't hear a thing but my heart. I glance over, and he has a straight face. I figure two can play this game. I mimic his moves except I brush my hand across the soft linen holding his rock-hard manhood captive. I circle his head with my thumb.

He chokes.

"You all right man?" Darius asks with concern.

"Nah, I'm good," he tells Darius, but his eyes are on me.

I look over, loving this game. "You sure?"

He drapes his arm behind me, but his hand crawls farther up my thigh until fingers brush my moist panties.

He leans in, the moment his lips feather over my ear I can't breathe. "Is this how you want to play this game, baby? If so, I got you."

"I'll keep that in mind."

He pulls back, but his body still blocks me from seeing anything but him. The fire in his eyes makes me throb with need.

"Well dayum take my girl on the table why don't ya!" Charlee says, and I don't blame her.

"Babe." Darius chuckles.

"I'm just sayin'."

I drop my head.

"Don't be embarrassed. You should want your man." Zach kisses me softly and sits back.

We hang out for hours telling old stories until close to midnight. But the hum running through my body only heightens the more I'm with him. Then we start the cleanup process.

Zach and I gather the paper products from outside. I place everything in a large trash bag. I turn, and he's waiting. His eyes follow me, and the intensity makes my knees weak.

"What is it? You're making me nervous." I joke, but I'm serious. The man knows how to stop my racing thoughts with a glance.

"I want to take you home tonight. But I don't want to scare you off again."

"I wasn't scared."

"Okay." He chuckles, gathering me in his arms. "Will you come home with me tonight?"

"You have a place here?"

"Yes. I lived here before moving back to Austin. I didn't sell my house since I always knew I'd come back." He caresses me before moving us back to the table. Charlee and Darius have kitchen duty.

"And your place in Austin?"

"I have it too. I usually lease it out. But I'm leaving it vacant for myself."

I wonder if I had anything to do with the decision, but I keep the thought to myself. We finish up, and he's waiting by the patio door for me. I walk over. He gives the area a final passing glance, then his eyes settle on me.

"Ready?"

CHAPTER 8

ZACH

I open the door to my sanctuary stepping back to allow Taylor to walk ahead of me. I inherited my house in Austin from my parents. But this house I entered into it blindly. It was a rebuild, and ultimately, I created a space that whispers home.

She saunters through the entry. I get a good look at her from the top of her faux dreadlocks to her burnt orange toe polish. She's wearing a crop top and a skirt flowing down to her sandals. The oversized colorful flowers look amazing against her brown skin. She is simply beautiful.

Taylor examines my walls. I arranged the front hall to feel like an art exhibit. My paintings line on both sides. I walk over and place a kiss on her shoulder. She tips her head up to kiss me before slipping from my grip.

Taylor takes one step, then another. Her eyes

roaming the art. A time or two, her hand brushes over the acrylic paints before looking over at me. The heat in her eyes shoots straight to my cock. I take a deep breath, trying to quiet the riot in my body. This is as intimate as sex.

Most people don't know these are my pieces.

Taylor does.

She takes a moment to examine each one patiently searching until she finds my name tattooed into the paint permanently marking my presence. The need to do the same to her body fills me. I need to make her mine.

Every time she stops, I slip over and touch her...kiss her. I can't keep my hands or lips off of her until we make it to the living room.

She faces me. "Zach, you are extremely talented. Do you plan to place your pieces in an exhibit?"

"Nah. Here is fine."

I run my hand across her exposed midriff until the fullness of her butt fills my hands. A soft moan escapes, and I treat it like a green light. I rub, and massage as my hands travel farther south. Her head drops back, and I kiss across her soft shoulder and up her neck until I'm nibbling on her earlobe.

"Let's finish the tour before I forget you're a guest." I step back, and her hand reaches out, brushing my cock. Need shoots through my veins like a drug. "Behave."

"I'll try." She turns to my open living room.

I take her hand and walk her out to my deck. "This

plot and structure were originally built in the 1920s. The location is unmatched with views of the downtown skyline, Bay Bridge and the bay. So, after leaving the military, I decided to rebuild it to what you see today."

"This is amazing."

I stare at her, agreeing. She's amazing. "Would you like anything?"

"Just you."

Her words end my quest to be patient, to take our time. I've already had her, and I want her again. For the past six months, I haven't touched a single woman because none of them were Taylor, and I'm ready to have all of her.

I kiss her. Not soft but demanding. I'm demanding, with my mouth, all the loving I've missed over these months. The more we kiss, the more I want her. I caress the curves of her body, reaching for the hem of her crop top. I toss it aside, and it lands on the couch, then I slip my hands beneath the waistband of her maxi skirt. I pull it lower to the floor, and her soft gasp fills the quiet room as I remain eye level with her heat.

"Are you ready, baby?" I ask, not taking my eyes off the prize.

"Uh-huh." I look up as I kneel at her feet. She shakes her head, pointing to my mouth. "You can't do that here."

I lick my lips then kiss the treat between her thighs

through the thin fabric of her panties. "Baby, I can do that anywhere."

"What if I fall?"

I can't help but chuckle as I stand. "Trust me, I won't let you."

I walk us, kissing her until she's against a wall. I lower her orange thong, brushing my fingers down her thighs until I reach her ankles. I glance up, and she steps out, one foot then the next. I reward her obedience with a leisure stroke of my finger over her pearl. She grips my head, and I gather her legs, bringing her up in the air. Her heat parting for me.

"Zach…"

MY BACK IS against the wall, and my thighs are wrapped around Zach's head as his tongue slips inside me. I can't hold back my moans of ecstasy. My body naturally thrusting into him. I don't last long as I feel release near.

I tell him. My hoarse cries filling the air, and he demands more of my body. His tongue has me pinned to the wall and his skills have me craving for more.

I pull at his hair and fire rips through my body. I see more stars than the clear San Francisco night sky can hold, and my body immediately goes limp. He lowers me, and we're face to face.

Is this what I've missed all these years?

My heart is beating at a cadence that makes me

want to get up, grab my clothes, and never look back. But his golden eyes won't let me.

I'm learning more about my body in Zach's skilled hands. I'm weak but eager. I'm tired but thrilled.

I grip his thick shaft in my hand, and he growls with pleasure. I stroke him spinning him around until his back is against the wall. I want him to feel the insane level of desire and passion and *love*.

I close my eyes tight as my tongue travels the length of his body. I can't love him because I can't give my heart, my love, to another man. This is about pleasure and pleasure only. Pleasure in tasting myself on his lips and the thrill of taking him in my mouth.

"Taylor…"

I take him stroke for stroke, trying to drown out the voice inside. *He's the one.* I take him deeper until I feel the veins of his cock pulse in my mouth and hear him scream my name.

We collapse to the floor. Zach shifts and pulls my body on top of his. The only sound in the room is our breathing. It was never like this with Les. I'm so conflicted. How can I remain in a relationship for almost fourteen years and not experience this?

It makes me doubt the love I had for Les. For all of his manwhore ways, I was in love with him once. But not anymore.

How do I even know what love is? I stayed knowing I should have left long ago.

I brush at the tear threatening to spill over. I can't

ruin this moment after waiting for months to find Zach. He just gave me the second-best night of my life, and I won't end it by crying over my years of ignorant bliss. But it wasn't bliss. It was hell.

To distrust the man I loved. To distrust him with my body or my heart. And now I'm giving my heart to a man I've known technically for six months, but I don't know him because we've only seen each other twice.

It's a rebound. Right? That must explain it.

"Why are you so quiet?"

I shake my head. The crazy monologue going on in my head must remain in my head until I get to my guys. They have to help me make sense of this.

Then I feel my body moving. Zach lifts us up, and I'm cradled in his arms. His eyes are beautiful.

"Did I hurt you?"

I shake my head.

"Did I push you too far?"

My eyes water, and I look away. "I'm pathetic."

"Look at me, Taylor."

"I can't." I cover my face, utterly embarrassed. We're moving, and I lay my head on his chest. His head rests on top of mine, and I snuggle my face into the warmth of his neck. He smells like a manly man. I kiss him over the rhythm of his heart.

I look over his shoulder, and we're taking the stairs two at a time. "This man is Superman strong."

"What was that?" His baritone voice rumbles through his chest and mine.

"Nothing." Now, I'm speaking my thoughts like Hunter, I chuckle.

"I imagine this is overwhelming," he says. "But I made myself a promise over the past six months. Hold on to my neck?"

I follow his instructions. He pulls back the covers and sits on top of his king size bed. His back is against the headboard and we are face to face.

"What promise did you make to yourself?"

"That I'd let you in. I've been hurt, Taylor. I'd reckon more than my fair share. And it made me hard and ornery. But there's something between us that time and distance couldn't kill." He kisses me. "I trust the universe enough to not chalk it up as a coincidence or as merely sexual attraction."

He has my attention. I lean into his strength. "What do you mean? How can you trust this…this…feeling? We don't know each other."

"Hell, I stopped trusting knowing people long ago." He laughs.

I sit up to see his face transform. I kiss him because I can't help it. "Keep talking."

"Yes, ma'am." He pulls the covers over us. "People show you what they want when they want. We all have moments we're proud of and others we despise. And both are usually accurate. So, everyone has the power to do good and evil, to love and hate."

71

I understand what he means. I've seen the good and evil in myself. My father. Les. And I guess one day I'll see it in Zach too.

"My solution is to sit back and let life give me what life deems I need," he says with such finality. It sounds like wacko talk to me.

"That takes guts." We share a laugh.

"I guess it does. But only if you sit around expecting it to take a specific shape and form. I don't. Instead, I let life surprise me, and I enjoy the ride." He wiggles his hips under me.

"All right lover boy, then how do you get over hurts? God brings this person into your life, they hurt you, then what? You wait for Him to take that person away?"

"No. I can't say I have it all figured out. I'm still working out the fine print. But I have a few clear examples, my ex-wife, my career as a Marine, and you."

"Me?"

"Think about it. I'm in a bar, determined to drown my feelings in booze and a beautiful woman saves me."

"I didn't save you." I sit up, looking into his eyes.

"You did. You wouldn't let me drink alone. You shared your beautiful body with me. You showed me there is still softness and wonder left in the world." I fall back against him kissing his chest, and Zach tightens his hold on me. I feel loved and cherished. "I could have been pissed. Why give me this amazing woman and let her walk off into the sunset with another man? Instead, we were separated for enough time that you could get over your situation, and I could get over mine. And here we are again."

"Thanks to the universe?" This is making more sense than I'd like to admit.

"The universe, God, fate, luck. I don't care about the title. The Being who is the giver of good things gave me you." He kisses my forehead.

"What if I'm not a good thing?" I don't fully believe the words. However, my past tells me differently. My father walked away. Les cheated until I had to walk away. Neither cared to look back and assess the damage they left behind.

Zach lifts my chin until our eyes meet. "You're more than a good thing. Try thinking about it this way, you had to experience that to have this."

"How do you know?"

"Because we're here, plus my gut says so."

"This is some technical stuff," I joke, and Zach laughs.

"I told you, I don't dig into it. I trust myself whether I'm wrong or right. And after six months of only knowing each other's names, I walk into a coffee shop almost two thousand miles away, and I find you."

"Okay. I give us that. But what about your ex-wife and my ex-fiancé and all the other bad things we've experienced."

"We need bad things to help us trust the good

things. Besides, what's the point of living if we can't expect good to come our way?"

I sit straight up. "You're either a genius or crazy."

"I'm equal parts of both." He laughs, and his golden eyes dance with happiness. "I don't have all the answers, but I'm certain that this is more than sex or attraction. The sex is amazing, and our attraction is undeniable. But together we can do more. Be more."

We talk for hours until the sun comes up. I see the beauty of the sun greet the day through his large bay window over his broad shoulder. We're lying on our sides facing each other.

His eyelids are dropping slowly. He's exhausted.

I can't sleep. My mind is running, running, running. I can't stop this train until I figure out where my next stop is.

His unwavering words float around in my mind. *What if the giver of good things gave me Zach?*

I watch as sleep takes him. I kiss him softly, careful not to wake him.

"What about love, Zach? Is it possible that this is love?"

"Yes, baby, it's possible."

I hold my breath. I can't believe I said that aloud and his eyes are still closed.

"How, Zach? How do you know?"

His golden eyes open brighter than the sun. His body covers mine. "I know because I love you."

I lean forward and kiss him. My heart knows he's right. But I'm scared.

"You'll see, baby. Just trust that things will happen when it's time."

Zach enters me. My body takes him in, riding the wave of the unknown. Kissing and touching and declaring the cloud of truth in our hearts. The bed rocks with every thrust. I scratch my pleasure in his skin and his release echoes to the depths of my soul until I give up trying to fight reason.

"I love you too."

CHAPTER 9

TAYLOR

*I*t's official, I'm a freelance coder. I completed the database for Platinum Prestige and for Delicious Chocolates. Then Zach managed to get me in on his project with Tech Secure. I know it's to keep me in San Francisco, but I've never been happier that I am now, and just when I try to fight it, it gets better.

"Look at you gettin' thicka than a Snicker," Charlee teases.

We're practically neighbors. It makes it easier, moving to a new city. We even had a delightful Memorial Day gathering at the house to celebrate Zach's father this year. I can't believe it's been a year since I met him.

"Like you have room to talk," I toss back watching her waddle down the stairs.

Charlee rubs her growing belly doing the Baby

Mama dance, and I laugh following her to the waiting car. Darius makes sure his lady is treated right. He arranges for three attendants to handle our private flight and a car service to drive us around once we deplane.

We are in Austin for our monthly meeting about Platinum Prestige. The guys are moving and shaking, so these meetings turn into a weekend of laughs, food, and catching up.

We climb in the waiting SUV, and of course, we're running late thanks to Charlee. We pull out our phones to call our men.

I smile at the thought of Zach. I've learned more about myself and love over the past year. I call him by video because I want to see him.

"Hey, gorgeous." He rubs at his eyes with the pads of his fingers.

"Hey, love. How long have you been on that computer?"

He laughs, leaning back in a cat-like stretch. "Since I dropped you off. How'd everything go?"

"It was a breeze, except we're running late." I roll my eyes at Charlee.

"Like they're starting without me." She sticks out her tongue, and I shake my head.

"Do you see what I'm dealing with?" I ask Zach, and he smiles.

"What you need to do is ask him to add his name to

the babysitting list," Charlee adds, pulling a sandwich out of her purse.

"What is that?"

"A sandwich. Want a bite?" She doesn't look my way. She's focused on peeling back the layers unearthing her snack.

"No. And why is it wrapped in a paper towel?" Zach laughs, and I can't believe she is eating the sandwich as crumbs drop to her much fuller breast.

"Heifas get brand new when they get a man. Like you ain't never ate a sandwich from your purse. And don't you lie, Taylor Mae Wallace, because I used to go to the movies with you." She dots the period with the end of her nasty sandwich. This is seriously some pregnant woman stuff because I can't recall a moment when the sight of Charlee has been more comical.

"And it smells awful." My stomach turns, and I dip my mouth and nose under the collar of my shirt, trying to filter out the aroma.

Charlee bounces her purse cuisine around in my face, and she's dancing. Zach has tears streaming down his face from laughing at the comedy show we're giving him.

"Wanna bite?" She thrusts it in my direction, and I swear I'm about to puke.

"No, thank you. Now please stay on your side of the vehicle." I flick my hand, and I mean it. She's laughing with Zach, but I legit feel awful. "What is it?"

"Peanut butter and jelly. You just tripping. You'd

think you're the one pregnant." She turns back to her sandwich, and her words are like a sinking ship in my head. I laugh it off.

I can't be pregnant. I can't have kids because my body can't.

But I've never been grossed out by peanut butter and jelly. I look at that damn sandwich and Charlee as I try to dismiss the warning bells in my head. Something tells me they're trying to alert me of impending doom as a laundry list runs like a cash register receipt.

I've been sick. Sleepy all the time. My boobs...I discreetly brush the side of my breast. They're sore. I turn to Charlee, and her Jedi bestie senses read my mind.

"Get the fuck outta here!" she screams.

"What happened?" I noticed for the first time that Zach isn't laughing. He's fully alert looking at me.

"Uh, nothing you know Charlee." I give her my best, *Don't say another word* look. "We're almost at S&J. I'll call you tonight when I get settled in." I try to rush him off the phone. But he's trying to read my mind, and I can't let him.

"Taylor." He leans closer to the screen.

"Welp, we're here. Love you. Bye." I disconnect the call.

"What was that?" She's not eating, and I'm fighting to control this situation.

"Nothing. I'm stressed with the new clients and extra contract work." I give a weak-ass smile. I can't be pregnant. Not after all these years. Hell, that's why I stood by Les because I felt as if my inability to have children had cheated him out of being a father.

"What's going through your head?" Charlee moves closer.

"Nothing." I can't say a word until I'm sure. "Promise."

"Are you sure?" Her concerned gaze makes me feel guilty for lying.

"Yeah. Now eat your nasty sandwich." I give her elbow a bump to push the sandwich to her mouth. Her eyes squint, and I look out the window.

But what if I am? Panic is threatening to spill out.

How can I be terrified and thrilled at the same time?

Thankfully, Charlee goes back to eating and calls Darius. While he's keeping her occupied, I'm having an internal breakdown because I've found the perfect guy who's doesn't want kids.

At all.

I watch the city roll by, and I'm numb, not knowing what to feel.

What if this universe of Zach's is giving me what I've always wanted? It gave me love. What if it's giving me a baby too?

I don't think it's possible. But I didn't trust it last time, and now I'm in love. So, instead of doubting, I choose to *believe what will be will be*.

I close my eyes and let my heart whisper a prayer. I lightly place a hand on my stomach.

Please let my womb carry the baby safely.
Please let the baby be healthy.

What about Zach? I can't imagine my life without Zach. I can't lose the man I love because of a miracle. God wouldn't let that happen. *Right?*

Zach always talks about the universe bringing us what we need when we need it. Well, I think the universe is smoking dope. Because it waits until I finally came to terms with not having children and I found a man who doesn't want them. It waits until I'm truly happy to pop this on me.

I drop my head to my hands. I've lost my mind for real. I have to turn my thinking around. That too I can attribute to Zach. He's always hopeful and loving, and when he decides he goes for it.

So I decide to see the good happening in my body. I acknowledge that God would give me this baby because I *am* happy, and I *am* loved, and it's not a one-sided relationship like before. But will Zach leave?

A lone tear crawls down my cheek, and I'm quick to brush it away. Glancing next to me, she's oblivious to my heart-breaking inches away from her.

Charlee bursts out laughing. Her head is back, and her feet are stomping. I can't hear Darius' side of the conversation, but I love love on her. Charlee wears it well.

I take several deep breaths as the SUV stops in front of S&J. Then I get a text.

Love you, whatever it is it's not bigger than us. I stare at the text message wanting to believe we are strong enough. But I'm just not sure. So, in the spirit of hope and love, I have to trust my love for Zach and his love for me.

I type, *Love you too*. Then I add the heart emoji.

We step out with our rolling luggage. In a matter of seconds, the guys surround us dancing in a circle. The distance has made our friendships stronger. We turn to head inside when Hunter places a hand on my arm.

"Let me talk with you for a second."

Oh no, can she tell? I'm silly. She can't possibly know because I'm not pregnant. We step inside and stop in the air-conditioned waiting area. The scent of the food from the courtyard assaults my nose, and I can't hold it any longer.

I take off running praying I make it to the bathroom in time.

I STEP out of the stall to wash my hands. I'll call my doctor tomorrow. This trip home comes at a perfect time. I walk out of the bathroom, and the guys are waiting.

I give them the same spiel that I gave Charlee. Harper slips her arm through mine, and Parker offers her place for us to hang out since it's crowded at S&J.

I grab a can of Sprite from the bar before we head out. I ride with Parker while the others order the food.

I volunteer to help set her place up for a mega slumber party.

Parker Belle Hamilton is one of the guys that gladly followed in her parents' footsteps. She's one of the top real estate agents in Austin. She owns property all over the city, and she's spreading her business to Houston and Dallas.

"You sure you're okay?" Parker asks as we get settled.

"Yes, I think I need this time at home to refresh and take a few days off. Can I get a tour of your mini-mansion?"

"Come on, and I'll get some more blankets."

We walk through her house. "This is definitely a place for entertaining."

"I doubt I'll entertain, but it should hold its market value and net me a nice profit when I'm ready to sell."

"Speaking of sell, could you help me find a place here?"

She looks over at me. "Everything okay?"

"Yeah, sure. I think it would be nice to have a place of my own. I could rent it out or something."

"Right." She nods, and it's like my inner turmoil is written on my face. "Taylor, secrets are acid to a relationship."

"I just need a few days to sort it out."

"How soon do you need a place?" The doorbell rings. "Hold that thought."

She leaves me alone, and I step out onto her patio,

and the sun hits the pool at the perfect angle. The rays of sunshine shimmer across the water's surface. The beauty doesn't outshine the calculation in my head. I've secretly had health issues with uterine fibroids and polyps since I started my menstrual cycle.

No one knows. Not even my guys.

I've never had surgery, and I've never been pregnant even after recklessly trying. Les cheated with the woman I call his ex when in reality he was sleeping with her for years. I figured who would want a woman that can't have children. So, I stayed.

The guys step outside, and I slap on my happy face. Tonight, I'll laugh and have a great time with them and tomorrow I'll face this issue head-on.

Alone.

CHAPTER 10

ZACH

"**M**an, you better be glad I'm your best friend," I tell Darius. Somehow, I've turned into his assistant wedding planner.

"Stop grumbling. I'll help you do the same." He laughs as we enter S&J. It's been over a year since Taylor moved to San Francisco. I stop looking at the bar. I can't believe I met her at that bar almost two years ago.

Time truly flies. We head to the conference room. Today we're meeting with the guys to plan Darius' surprise wedding. I've watched this man change in front of my eyes.

"I'm proud of you, D."

He smiles. "What brought that on?"

I shrug. "I've seen the changes in you and Charlee is good for you."

"She is, and now I'm about to be a father. I only hope I know what I'm doing." He nervously takes a drink of water.

"What do you mean?"

"You know exactly what I mean. We grew up without our fathers. I don't know how to change a diaper. I've never even held a baby until Hunter had the twins."

Kids.

It seems everywhere we turn Taylor's guys are having babies. Hunter, Harper, and now Charlee. The more they announce this baby shower or that I see her changing. But when I ask her, Taylor gives me that same fake smile. I'm fighting to trust her. However, her repeat trips to Austin make it hard to remain hopeful.

I turn to Darius. This is about him marrying Charlee and not me and my growing suspicions. "Don't worry about it. I think when you have your own kid, you'll naturally get the hang of it."

Darius glances around as if to ensure we are alone. "But what if I don't?"

"Then we'll go on YouTube." He stares at me in shock, and we laugh it off. "Don't sweat it, man. I'll do some research. There must be a new daddy class or something."

"Dude, thanks. Find it, and I'll go."

"And I'll go with you."

He taps our fists as the guys enter the room. I scan

their faces looking for my lady. I haven't seen her in two weeks. But she's not with them.

I look towards Parker since she sits closest to me. "Hey, Parker, where's Taylor?"

"She had a doctor's appointment. She should be here any second. Judging by your face you didn't know that."

"No." I sit back.

"It's probably a girly checkup." She smiles, but I'm not buying it.

"Excuse me." I head to the door.

"Zach man, you all right?" Darius stands.

"I'm cool. Start without me. I need to make a call."

I know Taylor's changing. It hurts because I know she's keeping something from me. I block out the nagging feeling that this is exactly what I think it is. But I don't want to put words to it. I don't want to give my past ground to kill my future. Not when I've done everything to make this relationship different, to make myself different.

I pull out my phone hitting speed dial before I make it outside. Her phone rings and I hear a sound in the distance. Naturally, I turn towards it. I see her heading my way, but she's not alone. I disconnect the call. She stares at the screen and drops the phone in her shoulder bag.

Taylor's fucking around.

"Trust her, Zach. Trust her. She loves you." I say the words as she walks toward the front door of S&J,

waiting for her to notice me. It's early evening, and the sun is setting. She obviously doesn't see me. The right thing to do is to wait for a reasonable explanation.

Rage causes my head to throb, and I don't think it's possible for me to hurt this much. But it is because I am. Because I've been here before...*I've been here before.* I spin away squeezing the bridge of my nose to keep my thoughts in check.

Taylor reaches for the handle, and I step forward. "Hey, babe."

"Zach." She jumps back a little. "What are you doing here?"

The words hang between us. The world slams to a halt.

"I'm here to meet with the guys about the wedding. What are you doing here with him?"

"Right." She turns to the guy standing back. Her eyes swing between us. "Zach, this is Les. Les, Zach."

"Les..." I step back. "Excuse us. I need to talk to my lady alone." I look at him. I see his calculating glance as he sizes me up. "Look, let me help you out. This isn't about you. But if you stay, I make it about us."

"You don't know me." Les steps forward.

"I know all I need to know. So, do yourself a favor." I step forward then I feel Taylor's hand on my arm.

"It's not what you think." Taylor's hands usually calm the storms in my life. But now I'm not sure of anything, and it's her fault.

I glance down. "How do you know what I think? It's

obvious I know nothing about what you're doing down here. Nonstop trips. Secret doctor's appointments. You show up with your ex-boyfriend. So, tell me, Taylor, what am I thinking right now?" I can't control the incremental rise of my voice.

"Don't raise your voice at her!"

"Zach, listen to me. I can explain." Her body is against mine, and I need space too, or I'm going to lose it. I remove her hands, and she grips tighter.

"Tae, think about the baby."

I turn towards Les and back to Taylor. "Baby...what baby?"

"Les, stop!"

"This day is getting fuckin' better by the minute." I turn to Les. "Touch me and APD will take both of us to jail because I could kill you with my bare hands right now."

"Listen to me, Zach. Look at me."

"Taylor, I can't. I never thought I'd say that to you or that you'd do this to me." I kiss her cheek and walk away from my life.

I drop my head running my hands through my hair. I hear her call my name. I grind my teeth, trying to overpower the ache in my heart.

I have to leave because I can't stay if she's cheating. And even if she's not cheating, she lied to me.

This is the type of trigger that will land me in jail or worse prison. I place one foot in front of the other, realizing this hurt is different. But some way I'll have to move on, again.

I love Taylor, but I promised myself I'd never love someone more than I love myself. And with every step, I pretend I want to know what it's like to live without my heart.

CHAPTER 11

*Z*ach won't return my calls. I disconnect the phone for the millionth time, not leaving a voicemail. Then I remember how good we are together. Before I lose my nerve and listen to my ego screaming, *Leave his ass alone*. I send a text message, *I love you*.

"What are you trying to teach me? What do you want from me?" I scream because screaming alone in these four walls is all I have. The kicking halts my fit. "I'm sorry, Junior."

His child grows in my womb. Every day my waist is an inch wider, my breasts are fuller. But I'm a high-risk pregnancy, and my doctors banned flying.

So, to protect our child, I do what I can to get through to Zach. I call, I email, I text, and he ignores every single one.

How long am I supposed to wait? When is it time to move on? When is it time to give up?

I see the hurt in Zach's eyes every time I close my eyes. Les saw me sitting in my car, looking at the ultrasound. Then he blurted it out in front of Zach ruining the surprise and my relationship.

"I'm fighting to save our family. But I'm tired of being invisible, Junior." He kicks, and it feels like, *Hang on, Mommy*.

I can't control the tears. It's like he knows I'm thinking about his father. I cling to knowing I'll see Zach tomorrow at the wedding.

After Zach's reaction to Les blurting out my pregnancy, I've kept it to myself. The only people that know are my doctors, my mother, Les, and Zach. I hear a knock at my door. I stand walking to it, I peek out, and like clockwork it's Les.

I open the door. "I really wish you'd stop."

"I got your favorite." He extends a bag of food.

I shake my head. "Les, stop doing this to yourself and please stop doing it to me.

"I'm not giving up on us."

"You already have." I feel a pain rush through my body. I grip the door handle. The Braxton Hicks started, and it's much too soon. "I need to lay down. Please leave and don't come back."

"But I miss you, Taylor, and I still love you."

"Love... What do you know about love? Does Jovonta know you're here every day? What about your kids? Are you thinking about your love for them right now?"

His face drops. "No, but I can't stop loving you."

"You already have. The moment you slept with another woman, and she had your child, your love for me ceased to exist."

"I love my kids, and I regret hurting you. I will never love another woman like I love you."

I shake my head. "Well, then you need to learn a different form of love. Did you ever consider how it broke my heart to see her have your child? Not once, but twice."

"And then you tell her about my struggles to get pregnant, so she can throw it in my face. This is how you love *me*. The woman who had your back. You sleep around like a whore, and you run back to me, begging for forgiveness. Well, love, don't live here. Not for you."

He steps back. The anger in his eyes shines like new pennies. Les is fine with his light brown skin and curly hair. I slept in his bed after he came home from being with other women. I washed the smell of his infidelity off his clothes.

And this is why I'm fighting to get my man back. Because I never once doubted Zach's love for me. Never. I see a car stop near the curb over Les' shoulder, but I don't recognize it. I'm feeling weak, and I need to lay down before the long list of duties tomorrow.

"Les, go home to your family. And if you love your kids, really love them. Treat their mother right. Give them what we never had. A mother and a father. I have to go. Bye."

Touching down in Austin drains the last ounce of energy from my body.

"I'll understand if you can't do this," Darius says on the other end of the line.

"I told you, I'd drag you down the aisle if I have to. Get off the phone. The fact that nosy Charlee hasn't figured it out yet is a modern-day miracle."

Darius laughs as the door to the airplane opens. He chartered this one for me and all the decorations and treats from Delicious Chocolates.

"Man, I need one more day, and I will be the man of the year."

"No doubt. Look, I need to run. I got some things to do before tomorrow."

"Thanks, man, I owe you."

"What did I tell you about that?"

"Yeah, yeah, yeah. One day you'll need to cash in, and I won't refuse."

"Bye." I laugh disconnecting the phone.

I start the process of loading the items in the waiting vehicle. I'm thankful for Darius' need to put together this secret wedding. It's kept me busy. But it hasn't kept the thoughts of Taylor away. Not with her calls, text messages, and voicemails. I listen to them every day and every night.

I beg Charlee to tell me how she's doing. However, being a true friend, she tells me, "Call her and ask for yourself."

The conversation we need to have can't happen by phone. It must happen in person. Walking away from her was the hardest thing I ever had to do in my life. And like a fool, I thought I'd move on. But everything in my house reminds me of her.

I can't sleep. I can't eat. I can't stop thinking about Les' words. "Think about the baby."

"Driver, I need you to make a quick detour."

I give her address. The moment the SUV rolls to a stop, I regret my decision to just show up at her place.

I see them, Taylor and Les, talking in the doorway of her house. But he's blocking my view from this angle.

I don't belong here, and I don't trust myself to see him again. I returned to counseling after the last run-in. I know she and I will talk but not like this. So, I'll have to wait one more day.

"Keep driving."

CHAPTER 12

"*I*s he here?" I ask Parker as she peaks through the glass doors leading to the courtyard. I missed the decorating, the rehearsal, but I can't miss the wedding.

"Yes, are you sure it's a good idea for you to be here?" Hunter asks, and guys gather around me.

"I'll walk down the aisle, stand as directed, then head back to my bed. But I can't miss this."

"What did your doctor say?" Harper grabs my hands. She's been concerned since I started having premature labor pains. We're due around the same time. But where her pregnancy has been a breeze, mine has been hell.

"Don't worry so much." I squeeze Harper's hands.

"He's signaling us," Hunter whispers.

We shuffle in order ready to walk out. Then I hear Harper whisper, "You'll tell us soon, right?"

I glance up. Harper's behind Hunter and in front of me. I nod. "I just need to straighten a few things out."

"Good."

Hunter opens the door. The courtyard looks like a dream. We each walk down the cobblestone path. We kiss Charlee's cheek as we pass and walk to our place at the flower-covered arch ahead.

I kiss her, and the tears are flowing. I'm happy for her and Darius. I follow the line of guys when I feel his eyes on me. I look over, and there's Zach. My heart stammers. His eyes are locked on mine.

He's lost weight, and I see bags under his golden eyes. I want to say something but now is not the time.

We turn facing Darius and Charlee as he drops to one knee. The guys huddle closer, passing tissues, linked arm, and arm. The area is filled with family and friends. Not a dry eye is in the room. I glance over, and Zach is staring at my stomach.

I can't hide it anymore. I'm almost six months, and we've had this dress altered three times. Out of instinct, I wrap a protective hand around my belly. I can't read his face. This will be the hardest conversation I'll ever have with him. Because I know he never expected this baby and the thought of him rejecting us twice is more than I can comprehend.

"Are you okay?" Parker asks.

She's to my left. I nod, but I'm lying. My heart is racing, and I'm trying to remain calm.

"I know you're lying," Parker adds. "And since I

haven't seen a doctor's note, I want you out of here as soon as she says I do." She leans over and kisses my belly.

My eyes start watering. "Stop, you'll mess up my makeup."

"I can't help it. You're carrying precious cargo. I'll make sure you have a ride, and I'll come by after we clean up."

"Yes, ma'am." I'm thankful for her and the guys. "Here she comes."

Charlee waddles over, and she hugs each of us, taking her time to make her way down the line.

"Are you okay with this?" She stops at me for a brief moment, then glances over her shoulder at Zach.

"I'm fine. Get moving. The man got you here on time, and you're still going to be late to the altar."

The guys laugh, and we push her forward to marry the love of her life.

I hear their pastor recite the words, and I've never had the opportunity to consider the vows made between a man and woman. I guess I never allowed myself to think that far. I couldn't get out of the funk of my own life. Happiness was this weird concept I never entirely understood, except for a season.

I glance over at Zach, and his eyes find mine after he gives Darius the wedding band. He and I never talked about marriage. The ringing of bells and the round of applause pull me from daydreaming. I pull out the bubbles, and we blow them around Charlee.

"I's married now!" she screams, and the guys go crazy. We take her into a sister-girl huddle, and the love is flowing. Happiness is flowing through the room. The smile on Darius' face is worth a billion dollars.

"It's time to dance with your husband," Hunter says.

"Bye, guys." Charlee gives a finger wave, and she's off.

"And it's time for you to head home. Let me get the driver to come around." Parker turns, and Les steps forward. "What are you doing here?"

"I can take her home."

I roll my eyes. "I can't believe you'd show up here."

"I told you, I'm not giving up."

"Your balls are massive right now dude. I need you to go before I have you put out." Parker stands in front of me, blocking Les' next move to reach for me.

I step back and bump into someone. I stumble and feel hands grip my waist.

"I got you," Zach says in my ear and butterflies flutter in my stomach. I exhale relaxing into his body.

Parker flags down a security guard, but Les doesn't stop.

"Look, I got you. Now you got me. Let's move on."

I watch as the guard grabs Les by the arm and Zach shields me with his body.

"Taylor, please."

"Goodbye, Les." I look in his eyes, hoping he gets the

point. "If you come near me again, I'll get a restraining order."

"Don't make it come to that," Zach adds.

The guard removes him. Parker turns to me. "You have fifteen minutes."

"Thank you." I turn to Zach. "Can we talk?"

"I NEED TO SIT." My eyes follow her hand as it cradles her stomach.

"Is it mine?"

Her eyes widen. "I can't believe you'd ask me that."

"Please answer the question."

"I will not." Her voice raises. "Because answering it will mean you believe I'd sleep with another man will being in a relationship with you, while I lived under your roof."

"No, what it means is I'm a man searching for the truth."

I reach for her, and she yanks her hand away from me. Taylor turns on her heels and heads to the building. I'm right behind her because I'm not leaving Austin until we fix this.

She storms past the guys, and I'm thankful they don't stop us. We reach the inside of S&J. She spins around, and I prepare for the holy hell she's about to rain down on me when she folds over.

The twist of pain crossing her face catches me off guard.

"Baby, what is it?"

"Aaahhhh…" Her knees buckle, and I swoop in to catch her before she falls. "The baby. Zach, the baby."

I cradle Taylor to my chest. "Tell me what to do."

"Take me to the hospital."

CHAPTER 13

ZACH

aylor is on a hospital bed. She's attached to machines, and the guys have gathered around like a wall of solidarity. I turn towards the sound of a squeaky wheel and see the nurse rolling in a machine. The doctor ordered an ultrasound.

"We'll be in the waiting room, Tae," Parker says.

"Can I stay?" I ask.

Taylor whispers, "Please."

I sit beside the bed. Her hands fiddle in her lap, and I gather them in mine. I kiss each one then I stand to kiss her. "It will be okay."

"Promise?" Her watery eyes meet mine.

"Promise." I don't know what I'm promising, but I'd give her anything. Any questions about my next move died the moment she collapsed in my arms.

The nurse pulls up her hospital gown, exposing Taylor's round belly. I lean over and whisper against her warm flesh. "I need you to fight, baby girl. Please fight for us." I kiss her stomach and feel movement beneath my lips. I look up at Taylor.

"*He* hears you." She smiles, but I still see worry there too.

I place a hand over her stomach and Taylor's hands cover mine. I feel the baby moving. "Does it hurt?"

"No." She shakes her head, and the ringlets in her hair dance around.

I laugh, and the baby moves again.

"Now he's just showing out," she adds.

The nurse waits for me to remove my hands. She squeezes gel on Taylor's stomach. Then seconds later, the sound of a train fills the room. I hold on to Taylor's hands, glancing around for the source.

"Have you found out the gender?" the nurse asks.

"Not yet. I have my next ultrasound scheduled for next week. Junior didn't want to cooperate last time." She laughs, and I see her stomach jump.

"Want to know today?"

Taylor looks at me. I nod, unable to speak.

"Yes, please."

The nurse moves the contraption around, pushing the gel around. The chugging of the little train is matching the beat of my heart. Then she starts pointing out body parts.

The feet. The little toes. The head. The heart.

"That's the train sound?" It's all so fascinating.

"Yes, sir. Now, let's see if we are having a boy or a girl."

I hold my breath. I turn to Taylor and whisper, "I don't care what it is…"

She nods and tears spill out her eyes. I stand and kiss her.

"It looks like you're having a girl."

I'm going to be a father. *A father!* My heart is about to burst out of my chest.

"I can admit you or release you with strict orders." The doctor comes in and places her on full bed rest. He wants to fight to keep the babies inside until she reaches thirty-eight weeks.

"You can release her. I'll make sure she follows your orders," I assure the doctor as I take down every directive and instruction.

"Your place or ours?"

"Ours."

I kiss her forehead. "I'll be back. I need to call ahead and get the place ready."

"Thank you." She looks relieved, and I plan to do whatever it takes to ensure our baby girl is healthy and doesn't make an early debut.

"I love you, Taylor. I want you and our family. Will you forgive me?"

"Yes, Zach."

I kiss her and the ache I've felt since the moment I walked away disappears. We are not perfect, and we have a lot to discuss. But we'll do it together.

I walk towards the door because I have some calls to make while they run the final tests.

"And, Zach."

I stop, turning back.

"She's yours."

"I know, Taylor."

ZACH CARRIES ME INSIDE, and I hear, "Surprise!"

I've held back the tears from being pissed, tears from being scared, and now I can't hold them back anymore. I cry, and not a regular cry, but an *ugly* cry.

Zach lowers me to the couch. He kisses the top of my matted curls. "I'll give you guys a few minutes. I need to start dinner so you can take your meds."

He leaves the room, and I wait for him to disappear down the hall. I look around, and all of them are here— Hunter, Charlee, Harper, Parker, Chase, Jordan, Payton, Alex, and Ryann.

"You're supposed to be off on your pre-baby moon."

"Not until I know you're okay." Charlee moves closer. "So, spill it."

"I'm pregnant." I open my arms in a ta-da fashion.

"This heifa is going to make me hurt her." They laugh at us both.

"I was told I'd never have children." The laughter stops, and I look at my hands. "I've had complications since junior high. It never reached the level of needing surgery, but I was told early on that kids were out."

"Is that why you stayed with Les?" Parker asks.

I nod. "Yeah, I stupidly didn't want to ruin his chance for having a child. But when Jovonta got pregnant the second time—"

"And that fool showed up at my wedding?" Charlee pushes herself forward. "I'm going to kill him."

"Oh no, you don't. We've had enough baby scares for the night." Alex plops down beside Charlee.

"And Zach?" Hunter asks.

"Les told him I was pregnant before I did."

"Daaayyyyyum!" The chorus rings through the room.

"Oh, he really tried it. He betta hope I don't see him." Charlee crosses her arms over her chest. "Why didn't you tell us, Tae?"

"I don't know. I was embarrassed. I was scared. Take your pick. I knew you guys had my back, but it seemed to spiral out of control. Then before I knew it, I was pregnant, which took me by surprise."

"Wait...the day I had the peanut butter and jelly sandwich?"

"Yes, you were right."

"Hot dayum!"

Hunter leans forward, and the guys gather around. "No more secrets. Tae, I know you're scared but don't ever forget that we are your sisters." The guys nod. "Come to us if you need anything."

"I will, and I'm sorry."

We huddle up, and I feel so much better.

"What can we do now?" Parker asks.

"Pray. I need this little one to stay put until at least thirty-eight weeks."

"Are you and Zach cool?"

"Yes, hearing about her from Les just added salt to an open wound. But we're going to do this thing together."

"Wait?! Her?" Jordan squeals.

"Yes, we found out tonight."

"Hunter, I think you need to branch out and open a daycare. Because y'all heifas are multiplying like Gremlins." I throw a pillow at Charlee.

We laugh and laugh until I can't cry or laugh. They hang around for a few hours until I'm exhausted and Zach shuts down the party.

They stand in solidarity, and Hunter steps forward. "Take care of her."

Charlee bursts through bump first. "Or I'll make you wish you were—"

"Babe! You can't threaten the man," Darius yells from behind her.

"I'm not threatening. It's a promise. Good night, sweetie." She kisses my cheek and waddles out with her husband on her heels.

He looks back. "Pray for me."

We laugh, and they disappear into the night. The guys leave one by one then Zach carries me up to our bed.

We lay face to face.

"Zach, I know this is not what you wanted."

"I told you from the jump that I wanted you. Kids, no kids. Crazy ex. Crazy folks. Crazy friends. I believe tonight I've proved it."

I laugh. "Yeah, I think you have. But what changed your mind?"

"Our daughter."

"Oh."

"Yes, and Darius."

"Oh, this is going to be good."

He pulls me across his body. My head is against his heart, and I'm home. I kiss his chest and wait for the story to begin.

"I went to a new daddy class with Darius."

My head pops up. "Oh, to be a fly on the wall. What did you learn?"

"We changed diapers, fixed bottles. I learned how to hold a baby."

"And this changed your mind?"

"Sort of. I realized I didn't want kids because I didn't know what to do with them. I've never been around kids. But the more I saw Darius preparing for his baby, the more I realized I could do this. I can be here for you and our baby."

He rolls me back, and I'm staring in his eyes.

"I knew if you could do it, I could do it. Plus, I missed the hell out of you."

I kiss him. Not sure how I got so lucky. I pull back. "The universe has done it again."

He laughs. "That and I decided. I want you for a lifetime, Taylor Mae Wallace."

"Good because I decided too."

His smoldering gaze makes me weak with need. "What did you decide, baby?"

"That I chose you. So, you're kind of stuck with us."

His mouth covers mine, and I feel the love to the soles of my feet. "Thank you for choosing me, baby."

"Thank *you* for loving me back."

EPILOGUE

ZACH

*T*aylor held on to thirty-seven weeks. She hated me every moment of the last two weeks because she was tired of staying in bed. But holding this bundle of joy in my hands made it all worth it.

"You want to meet your mommy?"

I bounce her around. I checked her fingers and toes. She has her mother's dark hair, and I think my eyes. But it's hard to tell.

We enter the room, and Taylor's eyes open. "How is she?"

"She's perfect."

I place our daughter in her arms. "I can't believe you're still crying."

"I can't believe I'm a mother. Thank you, Zach," she whispers, and it fills me with joy.

I kiss Taylor's lips, then I kiss my daughter's

forehead. I sit beside the bed, looking at the awe in her eyes. "So, what shall it be?"

We've been going around and round about what to name our princess. I'm leaving the final decision to Taylor.

"I have the perfect name." She smiles, looking up.

"Let me have it."

"Jessie Rose Russell."

My eyes burn and I glance away brushing away a tear. I stand up and cover her mouth with my own. "Thank you, baby."

"I think naming her after your father and my mother will give her an amazing start. Plus, she'll be an official second-generation guy."

"There's only one thing left to do."

"And what's that?" She pulls a little hat down over Jessie Rose's head.

"Will you marry me?" I drop to a knee beside the bed.

"Yes, Zach, I will."

My heart bursts with love, and it doesn't get better than this. "When?"

Laughter flows out of her, and my life is complete. "I think you're taking advantage of me while I'm emotionally vulnerable."

"I think I am too. Thought I better do it before the drugs wear off."

She covers her mouth to disguise the laughter because Jessie Rose is sleeping in her arms.

"Should I take it back?"

Her desire filled eyes met mine. "Don't you dare. I kind of think Taylor Russell has a nice ring to it."

"Not better than this."

I slide the rock on her finger, and all the jokes subside. "Oh, you trying to get some."

"It's official. No more hanging out with Charlee until after the ban on sexy time is lifted."

"Shut up and kiss me, man!"

I stand up, and I kiss the woman that turned my lonely life around.

"Break it up!"

Darius rolls Charlee into the room. Taylor and I laugh at our private joke since the woman in question is wheeled into the room with their baby boy.

"Proud of you, man," Darius says after looking Jessie Rose over.

"I'm proud of you too." I hold Little DJ.

We swapped babies and this little man is a big one. We laugh walking back to our ladies as the rest of the guys enter the room with their spouses and children. I sit in the bed next to Taylor, and she rests her head on my shoulder as Jessie Rose is officially introduced to her aunts, uncles, and cousins.

"You good, baby?" I whisper in her ear.

"I'm better than good. I finally have everything I've ever wanted." Her eyes glow with love, and I'm a lucky man. "I love you Zachary Russell. Thank you for asking me to get drunk in the bar."

"I love you too. But that story needs a remix. I plan to tell my Jessie Rose about the day I met her beautiful mother and that just won't do." I can't keep my lips off of her as the rumble of laughter and chatter surrounds us.

"I figure we have a lifetime to work out the details."

"Bet. Enough talking."

Taylor follows my request, and I thank the universe for changing my life and for finding my lady when I needed her most. The babies are passed around like accessories and the festive vibe of family fills the air.

I exhale and my joyful heart whispers, *Thank you.*

THANK you for reading **CHOSEN LOVE**. Taylor and Zach found their happily ever after. Meet the rest of her guys. Starting with Hunter and Ben's love story in *Platinum Love*.

I run to my favorite bar determined to figure out how I managed to lose my man and my inheritance in one night. The man is replaceable, but my monthly stipend is not.

I'm Hunter Preston. My friends call me Jo and I'm the only child to a media mogul. I was traveling the world, living my best life, until Daddy dropped a million-dollar bomb, annihilating my boujee world.

Double or nothing.

He gave me thirty days to pitch a million dollar business concept, or I can say goodbye to my trust fund. So, here I am with my girls, trying to get more than selfie advice, when Ben, the sexy bartender—who either abhors me or he's immune to my flirting—offers to help write the business plan under one condition. He wants $50,000. $50k to get $1 mil sounds reasonable until I remember how hot he is and how off-limits he is and how he wants nothing to do with a woman like me.

I'm screwed, pass me another drink.

One-click PLATINUM LOVE now!

AUTHOR'S NOTE

I said YES to a holiday romance writing project in 2019.

Ten authors. Ten holidays. Ten steamy romances. And we've all said yes to taking this journey together.

My ten stories are novella length. I think they're great for an evening of reading with your favorite glass of wine or tea. :) And I had the group of guys to make this series happen.

Then struts in Hunter and her squad, her guys. They came to me years ago. I love a good millionaire or billionaire romance like the next woman. But a few of my readers emailed me asking about a female millionaire. I thought why settle for one if I can write ten. **insert evil laugh**

I hope you enjoyed book one with Harper and Liam. Will you join me for the rest of the year as they build Platinum Prestige—one fly millionaire woman and hot guy at a time?

Don't miss a single release. Join my newsletter at **http://www.janesedixon.com/subscribe** to get updates and reader specials FIRST.

In closing, please leave a review. It helps others find my work and it keeps the lights on, if you know what I mean. ;)

I'll "see" you all soon.

Happy Reading,
Ja'Nese Dixon
www.janesedixon.com

P.S. Again, there are more Steamy Sensations Holiday Love stories available now. See them all on my website: http://www.janesedixon.com/steamy-sensations.

LEAVE A REVIEW

Did you enjoy *Chosen Love*?

Please leave a book review **HERE**. Reviews are extremely important and it helps me continue sharing my books with fellow readers.

JOIN MY NEWSLETTER

Be the FIRST to know!

Consider joining my newsletter? http://www.
janesedixon.com/subscribe Be the first to know
about releases and specials. You can unsubscribe
anytime.

BOOK 1

It's Valentine's Day.

I run to my favorite bar determined to figure out how I managed to lose my man and my inheritance in one night. The man is replaceable, but my monthly stipend is not.

I'm Hunter Preston. My friends call me Jo and I'm the only child to a media mogul. I was traveling the world, living my best life, until Daddy dropped a million-dollar bomb, annihilating my boujee world.

Double or nothing.

He gave me thirty days to pitch a million dollar business concept, or I can say goodbye to my trust fund.

So, here I am with my girls, trying to get more than selfie advice, when Ben, the sexy bartender—who either abhors me or he's immune to my flirting

—offers to help write the business plan under one condition. He wants $50,000.

$50k to get $1 mil sounds reasonable until I remember how hot he is and how off-limits he is and how he wants nothing to do with a woman like me.

I'm screwed, pass me another drink.

Get Your Copy on Amazon
or Read in Kindle Unlimited!

Read an excerpt on www.janesedixon.com.

BOOK 2

It's St. Patrick's Day.

The day is really not important, at least that's what I thought. I dress to impress, ready to secure my first contract as a partner with Platinum Prestige.

Simple, right? No, I wish.

I'm Harper Price. I've joined my best friends in starting an elite concierge service and I'm up. My sole task is to lease an airplane from Liam.

I walk in, he proposes, I walk out.

Apparently, his billionaire have gone to his head and now the sexy, arrogant menace won't leave me alone. His head is hard as a brick. (Take that any way you want.) And he refuses to accept "no" in any language. But I'm done with love.

No more.

Nada.

No mas.

Yet secretly, I'm scribbling my first name with his last name. Then he whispers, "Live a little Harper." And his money green eyes shine like dollars signs as he throws an unexpected curve ball. He'll grant three wishes, when…not if…I say yes.

Does having the most eligible rich bachelor begging to put a ring on it make me lucky? Hell no!

Not when my heart is screaming leap, my head is screaming caution, and my panties are.…

Oh hell, this is a f'in plane crash waiting to happen.

What is a woman to do?

Get Your Copy on Amazon
or Read in Kindle Unlimited!

Read an excerpt on www.janesedixon.com.

BOOK 5

What will it take to win his heart...again?

I couldn't see myself married until I conquered my career. So, when Maximus dropped to one knee in front of our family and friends, I freaked.

I'm Parker Hamilton. I should be experiencing an all-time high, as a partner of Platinum Prestige and a top real estate agent in Texas. But I don't have my man, and it's lonelier than I imagined.

So, I decided to host a soiree on a party bus taking my guests through Austin Hill Country, I don't expect to see Max board, especially with her.

She's the woman I've hated since she took kiddie scissors to my ponytail. The one who "accidentally" dropped fruit punch on my cream prom dress. The woman that finds a way to sabotage every picture perfect moment.

When Max looks at me, I can still see the hunger in his eyes.

Ready or not, I have four hours to make him mine again. And this time, I'm willing to do whatever it takes to get a second chance.

PreOrder YOUR Copy!

Millions of adoring fans dream of having one night with him, but only she has access to his heart.

Born with three commas in his bank account and melodies in his veins, Marques Carter is the rising prince of R&B. But not even his family name can guarantees success.

Brione Allen is a smart woman that made a dumb decision: trusting the wrong man. He blackmailed her family and now she's bound by a debt they knew she couldn't pay.

A chance meeting at his concert leads to an encrypted proposal: One week, one hundred thousand dollars, one incriminating secret. But when extortion and family ties expose them to the worst of the limelight, which secrets will they keep…and which will threaten their small light of hope?

**Get Your Copy on Amazon
or Read in Kindle Unlimited!**

CHAPTER 1

The same time every week for three years and the call got no easier. Brione Allen sat on the couch and blew out a deep breath. Dial the number. Ask for Kayla. But the knot in her stomach told the utter truth. Nothing about this was easy for her.

She tapped the numbers by memory, adding it to her favorites was something she couldn't stomach, not after all they'd done to her.

"Hello."

"Good evening Mrs. Bradley is Kayla around?" She stopped asking to speak with her hoping to gain a sense of control in the situation, but they held her captive with a vice grip on her heart.

"Hello to you too Brione." Her dusty voice held an air of censorship. "I'll call for her."

Kayla had a nanny, private school, and just about everything a little girl could want.

"Brione." She cringed at hearing his voice.

"Stewart, I was holding for Kayla."

"She'll have to call you back."

"But today is my—"

"Talk to you later."

The line disconnected and Brione screamed. No one heard her, and no one cared. Alone in her fancy plush prison, she'd gladly trade for their freedom.

She fell back on the couch and stared at the ceiling fan and her cellphone rang. She popped up anticipating the sweet sound of Kayla's voice. But the screen displayed another welcomed caller.

"Eliana Marshall. To what do I owe this honor?" Laughter flowed through the phone, Eliana was the only person she let close. The only person she trusted. The only person who knew the truth.

"Let's see…I'm your best friend. So I need no reason to call other than to hear your wonderful voice." Brione smiled. "Second, I'm flying into town, and I refuse any excuse you make for not seeing me."

Brione gripped the phone to her ear as she toyed with the hem of her blouse. She'd rushed home from work for nothing.

"I apologized a million times. But you plan to milk it dry," she joked pulling her stocking covered feet beneath her body and relaxed.

"I plan to milk it until it turns to powder if that will

get your butt out of that condo. I will *not* take no for an answer."

"Milk it dry *and* add in a level of guilt to the recipe."

"You got it." They laughed. "How are you?"

"I've been better." Brione looked around the room, furnished with the finest, reeking of their wealth. "You're heading here for the weekend?"

"No, I'm heading back indefinitely. Bruce and his wife are expecting twins, and they're keeping a close watch on her. We're planning to hang out in Houston until the babies arrive. Her doctor and family are all there. So, it could be a couple of months or longer."

"Yay!" Brione sat up, excited. "It will be nice to have you in town for a while."

"Just know I plan to pop up on your doorstep and drag you to a party or two while I'm there." Brione shook her head knowing they would have a battle ahead.

"How are you enjoying your job?"

Brione listened as Eliana shared her love of working for Bruce Daniels. She bounced around from Atlanta to Houston and back as his assistant.

"I can't believe the luck I've had with getting this job. It is stressful but fun. I'll be assisting Marques for a while too."

"Who is that?" The name sounded familiar, in a fuzzy, vague way.

"What rock do you live under?"

"The law school rock." She snickered. "I don't have

time for anything but class and studying. Well, that and my side gig."

"Side gig?"

"Eliana, who is Marques?"

"Oh, yeah. How do you *not* know who he is?" Her amazement was evident by the squeak in her voice. "He's a caramel dipped...tall, muscled...*god* in living color."

Brione lifted a brow at Eliana's description. "All that?"

"Yes, he's the epitome of sexy. Too bad he's my boss." She let out a sigh. "Anyway, he's an R&B singer from Atlanta. I guess you wouldn't know him since he's more underground." She was all business. "He is the flagship artist of Rockstar Entertainment. We're preparing to release an EP then his debut album."

Brione tried to picture this caramel sexy god. Her failed attempt morphed into her last dalliance that turned her life upside down, inside out, and left Brione estranged from her family.

"That sounds like a lot of work." Brione didn't listen to the radio and rarely watched TV. Her sights were set on securing an associate's position with a major law firm. Fun took a backseat.

"It is, which is part of the reason for my call." Eliana said.

"Oh, it wasn't just to hear my wonderful voice?"

"Of course."

"Yeah, yeah, yeah. Spill it, Honey." Brione walked to

the kitchen and opened the freezer, pushing around the contents until she found the frozen lasagna.

"Do you still help with events?"

"Yes, what's up?" She peeled back the corner of the lid and popped the plastic bowl into the microwave. Then she leaned a hip against the counter.

"Bruce's anticipated maternity leave and Marques' EP has opened a lot of doors for me. They've asked me to oversee the launch with hopes of promoting me to A&R."

"Congrats!"

"Thanks, but hold it for now. I still need to get through this project."

"So, basically it's an interview."

"Exactly."

"How can I help?" Brione dropped her head and chuckled at the faint sounds of Eliana's clapping. Eliana could make it happen without her, but Brione wanted to see her friend succeed. "I didn't say yes yet."

"But you will." Eliana blew a kiss through the phone. "I want to host a release party in Houston, and I'd love to bring you in. It pays good, and I'm almost certain I can get you the gig."

"Really? But I've never done a music event."

"Don't worry about that. Your work is impeccable, you're organized, timely, and you work well under extreme pressure. Are you free Saturday?"

"Yes, how about ten?"

"That's perfect. Get together your portfolio and let's

meet at the cafe on Saturday. I'll try to get either Bruce or Marques there too. That way I can cross two tasks off my list at once."

"I like the sound of that."

"You would, Miss Planner Chic. I maintain, where you thrive. One day, I'll grow up to be just like you."

Brione shook her head as if Eliana could see her. "No, ma'am. Grow up to be like you, and you'll be just fine."

"The thought of peanut butter and honey back in business is enticing don't you think."

"Houston ain't ready for us," Brione added.

Eliana's robust laughter rang through the phone. "Girl, if only they knew! And for totally selfish reasons, it would be a lifesaver to have your help *and* get to spend time with you without you skipping out on me."

They haven't seen each other in years, for one reason or another. But Brione missed her too. "I got you. When we're done, they're going to beg you to take that position. And I'll be there at 9:45 ready to rock n' roll."

"Awesome. I'll text you if anything changes. I gotta go, we're about to land." Eliana said.

"Be safe." The microwave beeped.

"I will. Love you Peanut Butter." Eliana giggled.

"Love you too Honey." They disconnected, Brione stood staring at the phone for a minute considering their long friendship.

Eliana was her roommate in college, their running

nicknames came when all they could afford was Ramen noodles, and peanut butter and jelly, except Eliana, liked hers with honey or syrup.

Music was Eliana's passion like organizing events was Brione's. However, she knew her love of centerpieces and tulle could not lead to her desired destination.

Brione gathered her hot food from the microwave and walked to the dining room, she turned into an office. She stared at the stack of textbooks. She entered law school for two reasons: money and time. The family connections between the Bradleys and her parents guaranteed her seat. But her high GPA landed her a full ride.

She cleared a space for her bowl, tonight she'd study and tomorrow she'd order pizza and work on her portfolio. She lowered into the chair in front of her laptop, placing her food aside. She opened the oversized law book and turned to the cases she needed to read and analyze for class tomorrow.

She leaned over the keyboard and forked a chunk of lasagna, she cradled her hand beneath it to keep the sauce from dripping onto her expensive textbooks. She popped it into her mouth and did a chair dance as the ricotta cheese and Italian sausage made her taste buds happy, momentarily overlooking that it almost burnt her tongue. She pushed the bowl back to let it cool and read the first legal case when her phone rang again.

The little face on the screen made her heart race with joy.

"Hello, Sweet Pea." Her voice trembled, she took a deep breath.

"Hi!" Brione could envision her chubby cheeks, full eye lashes, and radiant smile.

"I think this is the best surprise I've had all day." Her giggle warmed Brione's heart. "How was school today?"

Kayla talked about crayons and finger painting. Her new best friend and a boy pulling her pigtails. All the things Brione had to experience by phone and not in person. And as soon as the call started it ended, sending exaggerated kisses through the phone to the tune of Kayla's sweet laughter with promises of talking with her again on Saturday.

Life wasn't fair. That was too tall of an order.

Brione used the fork to cut into the cooler lasagna. She had stopped crying about it and questioning why long ago, instead she dealt with it, taking blow by blow and somehow managing to bounce back. But tonight she wanted to sit in it. From the sting of the scheduled phone calls to Stewart consistently dangling their freedom like cheese enticing a rat, reminding herself that she had a plan. This ache in her chest was only temporary.

One day she and Kayla would live under the same roof. Holding on to this goal kept her in one piece.

Kayla motivated Brione to work hard and she vowed not to repeat the same mistake twice. Men like the dreamy caramel sex god Eliana drooled over were bad news. Stewart was one of them. He walked into a room and every woman—married, single, it didn't matter—wanted him. She'd thought herself lucky.

Brione snickered at her foolish youth. None of them cared about what she wanted in life. Her goals. Her desires. To the Bradleys, her parents, Stewart, she was their pawn, their minion, their tool. *So they thought.*

She couldn't afford to crack. She ate the rest of her dinner, deciding to study first then get her portfolio together for her meeting with Eliana.

To get Kayla back, she needed money and landing the job with Eliana to organize Marques' event could be the break she'd prayed for.

CHAPTER 2

alking into Coffee Confessions had a ring of a homecoming for Marques Carter. He had spent many days hanging around waiting on Bruce to finish a shift before they went to the studio. Houston saved him and got his life back on course. Now that he was back, he hoped lightning would strike again for them.

He pulled the baseball cap lower to disguise himself. The release of his first official video last week gave him more than his usual double takes. In Atlanta, he couldn't go anywhere without people recognizing him, here offered a reprieve. But he didn't want to take any chances, welcoming the way people bumped right past him. It added another reason he loved being back in Houston.

Marques arrived early to meet with Bruce. He scanned the room, spotting a few empty tables and made his way to the line. He lifted his head to read the menu when he felt a soft bump behind him. He turned around and had to glance down at a petite woman.

"Excuse me." She held up a hand then reached out to stabilize a mug rocking back and forth on the shelf. "I was trying to miss the stroller and then the display and…" Her voice stalled as she finally looked up at him. Her lips parted in surprise. "Huh, sorry."

He chuckled. "I think I'll live."

She nodded without speaking as their gazes held. Marques let his eyes survey her light brown skin paired with jet black hair. It was curled softly brushing the sides of her face in a chic bob. Her heart-shaped face and doe eyes held curiosity as her full lashes brushed her high cheekbones with each exaggerated blink behind black frames. But when he zeroed in on her full lips coated with a hint of gloss, her tongue darted out and a groan reached his ears. He didn't know if it came from him or her.

"Andrew Carter." Using his legal name seemed appropriate as he extended a hand ready to see if her skin was as soft as it appeared.

"Brione Allen." Her smooth husky tone reminded him of a midnight radio jockey. The type of voice that held intrigue, mystery, and allure.

She accepted his hand and lightning passed from her touch through his body. *Damn.* Her eyes flashed to meet his as his heart rate tripled. He studied her thoughtfully, appreciating the heat lingering in the depths of her brown eyes.

"Welcome to Coffee Confessions, give in to your guilty pleasure. How can I be of service?" The barista behind the counter asked and Marques was at a loss for words. He still held her delicate hand in his thinking Miss Brione Allen was a guilty pleasure he'd gladly give in to. But judging by the penetrating stare she gave him as she snatched her hand away from his, he doubted she was on the menu.

"I'm sorry, I need a moment to review the menu. Brione after you." He extended his hand towards the counter and she stepped forward. She appeared as surprised as he was. The chemistry between them was as real as the nose on his face.

"Huh, sure." She stepped to the counter and tossed her purse on her shoulder like a barrier between them. *No, baby girl, that purse ain't gonna save you.*

She started to order and the sounds of the room faded into oblivion as Marques scanned the length of her body, the curve of her backside, and…

"And for you sir?" The barista wiggled his eyebrows. Heat rose to Marques' face, *caught*. But her hips were too tempting to ignore in pants that left no curve to the imagination.

"Our order is not tog—"

"Make it two of what she's having." He passed his credit card and turned back to Brione.

"That's not necessary."

"You're welcome," he teased, her expression much too severe for him.

Her eyes softened, "Thank you."

Brione stepped to the side and waited as Marques collected his receipt. They stood in heated silence both snagging discreet glances at the other waiting for their coffee. He had no clue what she ordered, thankfully he wasn't allergic to anything.

His senses were ablaze with her nearness. The closest comparison would be the moment he completed a new song. It gave the dueling emotions of exhilaration and exhaustion simultaneously.

"Are you off to work today?" He noticed the button up blouse and dress slacks.

"No, I'm meeting a friend. And you?"

"Business." She scanned his body in a sweeping motion. He wore a baseball cap with jeans and shirt. His goal was to blend in with the good people of Houston. He wished now that he'd given it more thought. Her mouth took on an unpleasant twist. "What you don't approve of my casual attire?"

"Oh no. I think it must be nice."

He searched her eyes and wished he could read her mind. The barista called his name for the order. Marques passed a cup to her and grabbed his own. The place was filling up quickly. He snagged a table and pulled out a chair for her.

"Join me while you wait." She hesitated. "Please." Brione slowly lowered to the chair. The floral scent of her perfume couldn't compete with the aroma of the coffee beans but it was a soft statement of her presence in the busy cafe.

Marques sat across from her finding it hard to contain the odd sensation in the pit of his stomach. He took a drink of the hot coffee to distract himself. The taste of caramel and whipped cream warmed his mouth. "This is delicious. What is it?"

"A custom drink. It's my favorite." She lifted the cup to her mouth and took a sip too. Remnants of her gloss left on the white lid.

"I'll have to get this again." He grabbed his phone and snapped a picture of the sleeve. "So Brione tell me, are you from Houston?"

She sat her cup on the table, pulling closer. Their knees brushed, her eyes widened. "No."

He waited for her to continue, she crossed her hands over the table. "Are you always this talkative?"

Her husky laughter rippled through the air. "No, it takes me a minute to warm up to people."

He nodded. Brione dropped her hands to her lap, "What about you? Are you from here?"

"No, I'm from Georgia."

"You said you're here on business. What type of business are you in?"

"I'm in a family business. I'm taking a little time off before we enter a busy season." It was obvious she didn't recognize him. It made him relax, he didn't feel "on."

"Do you travel often?" She asked.

"Not as often as I'd like."

"So you enjoy traveling?"

He nodded, "I do. It is a love of mine, I acquired it as a child. I traveled a lot with my parents." He took a drink of his coffee. He joined his father on many tours over the years. "The food, architecture, music, museums, I love all of it."

"Where all have you visited?" The warmth of her smile echoed in her voice.

He crossed his arms over his chest and extended his legs. "I visited, at last count, 40 or so of the great states of America. I've hit the tourist spots. Australia, Canada, South Africa, Rome, London, Egypt, I love it there too. Dubai, New Zealand, India, China, Morocco, Italy, Bali. There are more but you put me on the spot."

"Tell me about your favorite place." She leaned over the table and rested her chin in her hand. Her eyes bright and inquisitive.

"Uh…" her smile made it hard to think straight, he searched his mind, "I can't pick just one. My most recent trip was to Bora Bora."

"That place is on my wish list." A smile danced on her lips, heat coursed through his veins. *Get a grip!*

"Put a star by it. It is a place you'll never forget. The warmth of the water. Its vibrant turquoise color. There's something magical and healing about the island."

Her expression stilled and grew serious.

"Add this one to your wish list too." He wanted to see her smile again. "Torres del Paine National Park."

The spark returned. "Where is that?"

Marques leaned forward enjoying the light in her eyes. "It's in Chile. There's more sheep than people but the valleys are the most vibrant green and the sky the bluest blue you'll ever see. There is a small window when the weather is appropriate but it is worth it." He winked and something told him she mentally noted every word.

He wondered what she was thinking as she dropped her head, brushing her hair behind her ears. Her phone buzzed against the table and Brione glanced down at the screen.

"That's my friend." She held up her phone and finished her coffee. "We have to reschedule."

She stood from the table and leaned over to toss the empty cup in the trash.

"Would you like another?"

"No, I have studying to do."

"Studying?" He hoped to prolong her departure.

"I'm a law student." The glimmer in her eyes dulled.

"If I remember correctly there are three of them here."

"You are absolutely correct." She placed her purse on her shoulder and picked up a black portfolio. He missed that earlier.

"Would you like to grab lunch or something?"

"I really need to go." She shook her head and

glanced at her phone. "Thank you for the coffee and the conversation." An easy smiled played at the corners of her mouth.

"No, thank you for this wonderful concoction." He held up the cup shaking it.

"You're welcome. Have a nice day." She turned to leave and he reached for her arm.

"Take my number. I'm in town for a couple weeks. I *really* would like to see you again."

"I don't have time. I—"

"Take it…just in case. Pass me your phone and I'll enter it."

She searched his eyes for so long he thought she'd say no again.

"Okay." She hesitantly passed her unlocked phone, holding the top with the tip of her fingers, as if trying to avoid his touch.

He entered his personal cellphone number and placed the phone in her open palm. "I'll talk with you soon."

CHAPTER 3

*B*rione sat to study for finals, she had two weeks left before summer break. But his voice, his smile barraged her. "Study Bri!"

Thoughts of coffee with Andrew had her head in the clouds. The way his head fell back when he laughed. The twinkle in his eyes when he teased her. It was a chasm in time that passed too fast, she wanted more.

Closing her eyes she estimated his height was close to six feet, the outlines of his shoulders strained against the fabric of his shirt. He stood before her with his hands shoved in his pockets and a killer smile wide with perfect white teeth. His classically handsome features made him beautiful for a man.

People passed their table slowing to gawk at him, not once did he look away or acknowledge their presence. She wondered what his hair looked like beneath the cap but figured it really didn't matter. The man could be bald and she was sure she'd find him absolutely breathtaking—star quality.

Brione shook her head trying to rattle the images of him from her memories. But it proved impossible.

She tried reading the case at least ten times with no luck. But his soft encouragement, add this one to your wish list, rendered it impossible. Adding him to her list sound better. *Forget it.*

She opened her laptop and clicked on an internet browser. She typed in, Torres del Paine National Park and pressed enter. The results populated, her inner child didn't know where to start. She squealed stomping her feet beneath the table to release the energy. Pictures, she'd start there.

Brione clicked on "Images." The pictures before her eyes made her lean into the monitor. There were mountains, valleys, glaciers, snow, a winter heaven. What had he done during his visit? Did he hike? Was he alone? Was it as cold as it appeared?

She grabbed her phone and went back to his contact. And she noticed the note, Call me and let's have dinner sometime. She had stared at it for most of her *non-effective* study time.

She could send a text.

Her fingers hovered over the screen. No. She shook her head, and then what? He'd text her back and want to talk on the phone. She put the phone back on the table. Music. That would help.

She stood and turned on the wireless speaker, stopping by the kitchen for some water. Back at the coffee table, she sat in front of her textbook. She untwisted the top off the plastic bottle and took a cool drink. She scanned her phone for some music, pressed play and turned back to the case.

Brione read through several immigration cases for class. Her doorbell rang and she glanced at the clock. She wasn't expecting anyone, she never had guests except... She stood up and walked to the door and glanced through the peephole. Her heart dropped to her feet. *What is he doing here?*

Stewart leaned into the doorbell. *Ding dong. Ding dong. Ding dong.*

"I know you're there. Open up and stop staring at me through the peephole."

Brione jerked back, placing her back against the door. She cracked her knuckles and exhaled a shaky breath. Her palms sweaty, she looked down at her t-shirt and leggings. Her clothes didn't matter. But she felt more in control in a suit. Less like the young woman that fell for his smile and honey-laced words only to get stung by a wasp.

"You can do this Bri," she whispered running her wet hands down her pants. She clutched one hand in the other to still her shaking limbs. "This is your space. You are in control."

Ding dong. Ding dong. Ding dong.

"I'm not leaving." He stated.

She placed a hand on the handle and unlocked the bolt. She peeked through the opening created by the chain. "What do you want?"

"I promise this is not the way you want to handle this situation." He leveled his deadly stare.

"I'm studying."

"I guess Kayla will call you next week then. Give you time to study." He stepped back never breaking eye contact with her. She unlatched the chain, stepping back as he strolled in like he owned the place.

Brione closed the door. Stewart was like the boogeyman. People refute its existence until it pops up under your bed.

He sat on the couch and leaned back. "Are you always this rude to your guests?" He stretched his arms across the cushions, obviously comfortable. "Can I get some water, sweet tea, a sandwich? Damn." He laughed at his own joke.

"You didn't drive to Houston for water or a sandwich. So stop with the dramatics. What do you want?"

"What I've always wanted, *you.*"

Stewart Bradley knew how to pop up on her doorstep when she felt confident, when she finally decided to not let him push her around, then she emerged from the shadows to call her bluff.

"Have a seat? I won't bite."

The invisible shackles clanked around her ankles as she sat in the chair closest to the door. "What do you want Stewart?"

"How are you?" His eyes scanned her body. She wrapped her arms protectively around her waist.

"I'm fine."

"When did you cut your hair and what's up with your clothes?"

"Stewart I'm studying." His mother was always dressed to perfection including a string of white pearls. He wanted a clone of Mrs. Bradley, the thought of her old sweats and short hair irking him brought a smile to her face. "And I like my bob."

"Is this how you're carrying yourself nowadays?"

"Is that why you visited? If so, we can end this conversation here and now." She swallowed hard.

"Don't let law school go to your head. This is still my show."

"Why don't you move on and let us move on too?"

"There is no *us* without me," he growled. "You got into law school because of me. You can't care for Kayla without a job. What about her education? Her tutors? Her nanny? And don't forget about your pops." His glare intimidating. "I will deliver his career in a wastebasket. Is that what you want? Do you want to ruin everyone's lives because of your selfishness?"

The boogeyman live and in living color. Panic was

rioting inside her gnawing away at her confidence. Gnawing away at her plans and dousing her hope.

She once trusted this man and thought he loved her. That was the face of love. It was laughable. Her tongue felt thick and her nerves made it hard to form a coherent thought. She was tired of him pushing her around.

Don't let him push you around. Brione couldn't trust that voice, hadn't she invited him into her life in the first place. She dropped her head, stirring uneasily in the chair, hoping to hide the shame from his probing eyes. It was the cost of trusting an untrustworthy person. A person who valued self-ambition and greed over people. *How had I missed it?*

"Are you done playing with me?" His nostrils flared with fury.

She nodded, fear splintered her heart.

"Good." The storm clouds left his eyes. "Mom wants us to set a date."

She squeezed her eyes shut gripping the arms of the chair. "Stewart you don't want to marry me. We have nothing in common—"

"Nothing in common? We have *everything* in common. Let me shoot it to you straight. I want a date or so help me, Brione Allen, I'll bury you and your father's dreams of sitting in the Oval Office. And I'll ensure you never ever see our daughter again." He ground the words out through clenched teeth. "Understand?"

"Yes."

Continue Reading...

**Get Your Copy on Amazon
or Read in Kindle Unlimited!**

.

Blazin' Love (Contemporary Romance)

Platinum Love

Privileged Love

Exclusive Love

Chosen Love

Special Love

Conspiracy Ink Series (Romantic Suspense)

Veiled Conspiracy (re-release Summer 2019)

Forbidden Chords Series (Contemporary Romance)

Rockstar Secrets (Book 1)

Rockstar Sinners (Book 2)

Rockstar Savages (Book 3)

Precious Stones Series (Romantic Suspense)

Before Black Diamond (Prequel)

Black Diamond (Book 1)

African Emerald (Book 2)

Fire Opal (Book 3)

Ready for Love Series (Sweet Romance)

Caramel Surprise (Book 1)

Love's Hope (Book 2)

Hidden Desire (Book 3)

Ready for Love Boxed Set (Books 1 - 3)

Smith Pact Duo (Contemporary Romance)

Yuki's Luck (Book 1)

Tempting Asher (Book 2)

Smith Surprise (Book 3)

See all of my books on my website:

http://www.janesedixon.com/books.

HOLIDAY LOVE

10 Authors. 10 Holidays. 10 *Steamy Romances*.

Ten romance authors bring you a sexy story to fire up your holiday. Each author has their own series in 2019 with one thing in common - Holidays!

Check out all of the Steamy Sensations books HERE or my website janesedixon.com/steamy-sensations!

ABOUT THE AUTHOR

Ja'Nese Dixon pens tales of romance in several sub-genres. But her favorites are the ones that manage to keep readers sitting on the edge of their seats lying to themselves about reading "just one more chapter".

Ja'Nese is an avid reader and coffee drinker, who also loves to run, cook, and craft. Her ultimate goal as a writer is to give you a little "staycation" with every story. And she aims to make this present story no exception. Sit back, grab a snack and enjoy.

Ja'Nese calls Houston home with her husband, three kiddos and a four-legged diva dog.

Visit her website at www.janesedixon.com if you enjoy romance, suspense and good stories.

Subscribe to Ja'Nese Newsletter "Reader's Staycation" for reader exclusives, regular giveaways and more.

Stay in Touch:
www.janesedixon.com
info@janesedixon.com

facebook.com/AuthorJaNeseDixon

twitter.com/janesedixon

instagram.com/authorjanesedixon

amazon.com/author/janesedixon

bookbub.com/authors/ja-nese-dixon

ABOUT THE PUBLISHER

Purpose Prevails Publishing
2231B Center St. STE 144
Deer Park, TX 77536
www.purposeprevailspublishing.com

www.ingramcontent.com/pod-product-compliance
Lightning Source LLC
Chambersburg PA
CBHW020129180626
46810CB00004B/1472